THE FRENCH ENCOUNTER

WINDOW TO THE HEART SAGA

JENNA BRANDT

CONTENTS

DESCRIPTION

Window to the Heart Saga: a recountal of the epic journey of Lady Margaret, a young English noblewoman, who through many trials, obstacles, and tragedies, discovers her own inner strength, the sustaining force of faith in God, and the power of family and friends. In this three-part series, experience new places and cultures as the heroine travels from England to France and completes her adventures in America. The series has compelling themes of love, loss, faith and hope with a exceptionally gratifying conclusion.

The French Encounter (Book 2). Ruined by a night she will never forget, Lady Margaret, Countess of Renwick, must flee from England with her infant son to hide from the man who destroyed her life and from the sister-in-law who hates her. Relentlessly, the duke and viscountess hunt for them, planning to take the child to whom they both feel entitled. Margaret turns to God, believing he will protect her family and help her find her long-lost twin brother, Randall. While searching for Randall in France, Margaret is pursued by two enticing men: Pierre, the alluring Vidame of Demoulin, and Michel, the powerful Marquis de Badour. One man promises passion while the other offers security. Will Margaret surrender the chance for love to secure her safety?

While fleeing from danger and searching for her long-lost brother, Lady Margaret encounters new love. Despite her past, can Lady Margaret discover hope for the future? Deeply passionate and intensely gripping, **The French Encounter** weighs the struggle between giving in to temptation and sacrificing for refuge.

Window to the Heart Saga

Book 1: The English Proposal
Book 2: The French Encounter
Book 3: The American Conquest

For more information about Jenna Brandt, visit her on any of her websites.

www.JennaBrandt.com
www.facebook.com/JennaBrandtAuthor
www.twitter.com/JennaDBrandt
www.amazon.com/author/jennabrandt
Signup for Jenna Brandt's Newsletter

To my husband, Dustin.
We have shared numerous moments of joy and loss,
and through it all, you have been my anchor in the storm.
Here is to twenty years of love and friendship.
Looking forward to twenty more.

CHAPTER 1

1863 Le Havre, France

*L*ady Margaret, Countess of Renwick and widow of Henry William Wiltshire, the Viscount Rolantry, held on to the rail of the steamboat. As she approached the French shoreline, her long, raven locks blew in the wind and she could feel the fall air on her pale skin.

As she clutched the vessel's edge, she wondered what lay ahead for her. Not only was she afraid, since it was her first time on the open sea, but also because everything was so unknown. She had barely been out of her province in England, and now she was about to step foot in a foreign country. This new place held the possibility of a completely fresh future for her and her newborn son.

She never thought she would leave her homeland of England, let alone run away in the middle of the night because she feared for the safety of her family. But with her parents dead and having no family to protect her, she had no other recourse.

The events that led to her fleeing to France still haunted her. She would never forget the brutal attack on her body by Richard Charles Crawley III, the Duke of Witherton, or how he set the whole ordeal in motion to look like she willingly betrayed her husband. The horrified look of anguish on Henry's face when he saw what seemed to be an unfaithful liaison would not leave her. She had tried to convince him it was not her doing and that she had been trying to protect him because she loved him, but he did not believe her when she told him that the duke had tricked her so he could use her to hurt Henry.

So much mistrust and damage had been done by her naïve belief that she had been in love with the duke that, by the time she uttered the words out loud, saying "I love you" could not fix what had been destroyed. Her husband died in a duel over her honor, believing she never loved him. Margaret could not reconcile her guilt from his death.

As punishment, her late husband's sister, Catherine, enforced the banishment Henry had placed on her, confining her to their London estate. In an ironic twist, two months into her exile, she found out that she was with child. It was only her faith in God and her choice to live for her unborn son that made it possible for Margaret to survive.

Every day had been a battle to live without the love of her life. Basic things like eating and sleeping felt like impossible feats. And the most difficult part was living in fear of the outcome of the paternity of her son. She recalled Catherine saying to her, *"Once the baby is born, I will come back and make the decision of what will be done with it. You better hope and pray that it is Henry's child, because if it is not, you will have to figure out how to survive on your own. Additionally, there is the possibility that the duke will want to lay claim to his bastard."*

But God protected her. Through her exile, she was given the opportunity to plan her escape. When she gave birth to her son, whom she named Henry after her late husband, she was able to keep Catherine from intercepting her and carrying out her plans.

Even though she had never been to France, Margaret knew more about it than any other country. Her twin brother, Randall, had been lost at sea when his ship went down outside of France. She had vigorously researched everything there was to know about the country, hoping that one day she might be able to take a trip to France to find him. But her father dealt with Randall's presumed death by focusing on anything other than finding out what happened to him, which left no room to allow her to pursue her hopes of finding her brother alive.

Flash forward eight years and Margaret had finally made it to France in the most unexpected way. When she decided to flee the country, she made the decision to go there so she could carry out her long-hidden plan to search for her brother. If she had to leave behind everything she loved and knew, it was not going to be in vain. If her brother was alive, she was going to find him.

As Margaret stepped off the ship, she was greeted by a tall, well-dressed gentleman with a thick French accent. "Welcome to France, Countess. I am so delighted to see you again. I am glad that you have arrived safe, and I have arranged for you to stay at my estate."

Pierre Girard, the Vidame of Demoulin, was an old family friend and had visited her family right before her marriage to Henry. He had approached her father to discuss the possibility of courting her, but her father had declined his offer, opting to keep his promise to Henry's late father instead.

Margaret studied the vidame; he had a chiseled body that was made evident by his tailored, stately suit in light grey. He was quite handsome with his straight, jet-black hair that stood out in contrast against his pale skin. His face was set off by his dark brown eyes that drew her in and held her attention. He was confident but not arrogant, which was refreshing in a nobleman, and there was something about him that exuded sensuality.

She had not been able to see Pierre's admirable qualities when he previously visited because she had been infatuated with the Duke of Witherton. Nothing else mattered to her, and she had no idea who the duke really was or of what he was capable.

When Margaret realized she was in danger from two different directions, she knew she had to leave England to protect her son. She discreetly contacted the vidame, via letter, to ask if he would be willing to allow her to stay with him while she made more permanent arrangements. She explained her travel and stay with him should be kept quiet as there were safety concerns for her family if they remained in England. The vidame had agreed to her request, and Margaret was relieved to find somewhere safe to stay while she figured out what to do next.

"Countess, by title I am a protector of land and people alike. I assure you that you will be safe and I will not allow any harm to come to you or your son while you are under my care." The young man bowed deeply, and as he came up, he took Margaret's hand and kissed the top of it.

She smiled softly at him and spoke in flawless French, "Thank you for your hospitality, my lord."

His mouth formed an appreciative grin. "You speak French beautifully, Countess. Tell me, how is it that you came to speak my language so fluently?"

"I had a deep... interest in your country since I was a young child and wanted to know every detail about it, including how to speak the language. At my insistence, my father hired a French tutor."

He took her hand and put it in the crook of his arm. "Come, I will escort you to my estate, and then we can discuss what your plans shall be while you stay with me."

"I am honored that you have done as much as you already have for us. I am truly grateful."

"After our last encounter in England, you should know by

now that I would do anything you ask of me."

She blushed at the compliment. It seemed Pierre's interest in her had not dissipated since the last time they were together. "Your generosity is just one of your numerous admirable qualities, my lord."

Hearing a noise behind her, they both looked at her entourage. With a hint of mirth, Pierre commented, "It does not seem you travel light, Countess."

Margaret looked at her devoted servants, Albert, Sarah, Motty, and Francisca, who chose to follow her to France. Along with her son and several pieces of luggage, she could see that she appeared to be ostentatious. However, what the vidame did not know was that this trip had no return date. There was no going home for any of them.

As they walked towards the nearby carriage, Margaret weighed her options on whether to tell the vidame the full details of her predicament. She worried that, if she told him the entire circumstances surrounding her sordid past, he would look at her differently. She did not think she could handle another person judging her for something that was out of her control. She needed the vidame to remain on her side, so she chose to keep the intimate details surrounding her reasons for coming to France private.

"I hope that France meets and exceeds all of your expectations," the vidame said as he helped Margaret up into the carriage.

She turned her head and looked down at him with her deep violet eyes, replying, "I am sure that it will, my lord."

CHAPTER 2

The vidame's estate was expansive, one of the biggest in which she had ever been, and she thoroughly valued all the comforts. It had been a long time since she had been treated so well. When Henry died, Catherine had left her with a skeleton staff and a small stipend for her needs. She had saved almost all of it, along with the hidden money she had from her father's safety deposit box, for her plan to flee England. She had spent the entirety of her pregnancy living like a pauper.

"So, how are you settling into Parintene? Do you approve of my home?"

Margaret took a sip of her wine and then replied, "Yes, Pierre, it is lovely."

The two of them had grown acquainted over the two weeks she had stayed at his home and started calling each other by their given names.

"I believe that we are friends again, like we were as children. Do you agree?"

Smiling, she nodded. "We are fast becoming that, I agree. I cannot thank you enough for taking us in like this. I have not felt this secure in almost a year's time."

"I am pleased you feel safe. I also hope you are enjoying the amenities."

"Most assuredly. Your home provides a myriad of activities. As you may have guessed, the stable is my preferred destination."

"I ascertained as much from my previous visit to your home. I remember you wearing that lovely riding habit and knew you would be partial. I am glad the stables are to your liking. I had them refurbished for your arrival, as well as purchased additional horses for your use."

Margaret was impressed by Pierre going to such a prodigious extent to make her stay agreeable. She found it soothing being in the stables, as she had always found comfort in riding horses.

"I appreciate your care in providing such lavish accommodations. Your stables are magnificent and the horses are wonderful. However, I miss my own horse, Charlie, terribly."

Charlotte's Pride—or Charlie, as Margaret called her—was the Arabian filly her family had been working towards preparing for show in England before everything went awry in her life. Margaret had spent countless hours in the stables making sure the trainers did everything right. As a woman, she was unable to do the work herself, but she had read comprehensively on the subject and participated as much as possible. Her father had allowed her to make most decisions in regard to their estate horses, and her late husband had given her the same latitude with the ones they owned. But when she had fled, she was unable to take most of her possessions with her, and a horse was out of the question. Giving up so much, Margaret wanted one day to be able to reclaim part of her hopes and dreams by producing her own line of purebred horses. She yearned to find the finances and land to do it, but all of that would have to wait until she found her brother, if in fact he was still alive. If she did, they could move away together, somewhere remote where no one would ever find them.

"I am sorry you were unable to bring her with you. I know how much you cared for her."

Margaret looked away and tried to hide her sadness at the thought of never seeing Charlie again. "Thank you. It has been difficult coping with the many losses."

Pierre had proven a faithful and devoted confidant, and she knew that keeping her past from him would not serve either of them well. He could not help protect her if he did not know from whom he was doing the protecting, so Margaret had explained her entire situation to him—at least, the broad strokes of it. She still could not bear to discuss the details with anyone. The pain and humiliation felt as fresh as it did the night the duke forced himself on her.

"I am glad that your father was friends with mine. If not, my son might be in the clutches of someone else by now."

He frowned. "You are sure that you do not want me to help you with your situation? I know many influential people who could take care of your *problem* for you. You would not have to worry any longer."

She shook her head. "This particular situation is something that will not just go away simply by contacting the right person."

Margaret watched as Pierre smirked and raised an eyebrow, as if amused. He then stated, with a hint of danger in his voice, "I would argue it depends upon the person you contact. There are many types of people in this world, and I know the right types that could make both of your problems disappear."

She realized immediately that he meant he could make the duke and Catherine "disappear." Though tempting, she could not be responsible for the death of another human being, even one as vile as Witherton or as hateful as Catherine. Her new relationship with God made her value all human life, and she truly believed in the idea that anyone could be saved. It was hard to accept that meant even the duke, but at the core of her beliefs, she truly believed everyone was salvageable. It was not her business to save them, but it also was not her place to remove the chance of redemption. She left justice for the Lord to exact one day and preferred to focus on her future.

Uncomfortable with the conversation, Margaret changed the topic. "There *is* something else with which you can help me. I am in need of hiring an investigator. Could you help me locate one?"

Pierre leaned back in consideration for a few moments before replying, "I have used one on occasion myself. The one I employ is exceptional, as well as quite discreet. I can set up an appointment with him whenever you wish. But I ask you, why is it that you need to hire one, Margaret?"

She stared at the wineglass and absentmindedly tapped the stem with her fingertips. After a few moments, she looked over at Pierre. "I need to find my brother."

He furrowed his brows together in confusion. "I do not understand what you mean. I was under the impression that you had no family left. I had been informed of your father's death, and I went to school with your brother Randall before he was killed."

"No, Pierre, I know Randall never died in that shipwreck. If he had, I would have felt it. We have a special bond as twins, and I just know that he is still alive." She glanced over at the window and continued as she stared out. "Randall is one of the main reasons I came to France. I have wanted to search for him for years but have never been able to leave England. You might think that I am on a fool's errand, and you might even be right, but I have to know for certain." She brought her focus back to Pierre. "Since I am here now, I need to try to find him. He is the only family I have left."

Pierre gestured to one of the servants, who immediately came to his side. He whispered something in the servant's ear and then turned his attention back to Margaret.

"I just sent word to Josef Mulchere. He will help you find your brother."

"Thank you again, Pierre."

"I understand your reason for coming here now, but I have to admit I had hoped, before your disclosure, that you chose to come to France because of me. You know I had been interested in pursuing a courtship with you before you married Henry. My feelings for you have not altered."

"You are a dear friend, Pierre, but I am not ready for a romantic relationship. I am still in mourning over Henry's death."

Pierre nodded. "I would expect nothing less, but when you are ready, I will be waiting."

Margaret's smile faded and a pang of sadness took hold in her. "You should not wait for me. I am in no condition to be with anyone. I fear I am broken beyond repair."

"You give entirely too much power to *that* man. The duke did not destroy you. The woman who sits before me is kinder, wiser, and stronger than the one I knew back in England."

"You have always seen the best in me, Pierre, even when we were children. When I see you, I think of happier times, when you and I, along with Randall and Henry, played in the family gardens. Life was so much easier back then. So much loss has occurred since those days."

"You have had more than your fair share of misfortunes. I do, indeed, hope you find your brother. I think it would do the both of us a world of good. When he was lost, it was one of the hardest times in my life, and I know it was for you as well."

"Randall's disappearance left a hole in all our lives."

"Agreed, but there is hope he can be returned to us. If he is alive, Monsieur Mulchere will find him."

The vidame had great pull, and by the next morning, Margaret found herself meeting with one of the best investigators in all of France.

"Good afternoon, my lady. I am Josef Mulchere." A man of average height and build, with an exceedingly unremarkable face, which most likely served him well in his line of work, bowed graciously. "How may I be of service to you?"

"I need you to make inquiries about someone for me."

"Whom will I be inquiring about?" asked the elderly man with slicked back grey hair.

"My twin brother, Randall, heir to the Earl of Renwick title."

"Very good, my lady, but if it pleases you, I will need to know some information about him."

"I will answer any questions you may have. I am willing to do whatever it takes to locate him."

"What is his full name?"

"Randall Thomas Wellesley."

"When was the last time you had contact with him?"

"Eight years ago. He was coming home from boarding school here in France when the ship he was traveling on was lost at sea during a storm. He was presumed dead, but a body was never found."

Mulchere continued to write down the answers that Margaret provided and occasionally made a barely audible "hmm" under his breath.

"What made them assume he was dead?"

"They found a shirt near the debris from the shipwreck. It had his monogram on it and it was... torn apart." Recounting the events surrounding the loss of her brother was still difficult. She rarely talked about it, but she forced herself to continue. "The authorities believe he was killed by sharks and that is why there was no body to recover."

Margaret's eyes began to tear up in the corners, and she could see the look of empathy on the detective's face. "I am sorry, my lady. I do not wish to trouble you with these questions."

"I understand that you need as much information as possible for the best chance of locating my brother."

"I do. If it is bearable, may I ask you a few more questions?"

"Certainly."

"What was the name of the ship on which your brother was traveling?"

"The Wandering Stranger."

"And what was the captain's name?"

"William Sanders. They found his body along with several others."

"Where there any known survivors?"

"They pulled one person from the wreckage. His name was George Bishop, a deckhand on the ship."

"Did they ever talk with him about what happened when the ship went down or what he saw during the events surrounding the shipwreck?"

"Yes, they did interview him. Unfortunately, due to a severe head wound, he could not recall any details."

He made another "Uh-huh" sound under his breath and stated, "I believe I have enough information to start my investigation. If I have any additional questions, I will be in contact."

Margaret smiled gratefully at the detective and said with urgency in her voice, "Finding my brother is of the upmost concern to me, Monsieur Mulchere. Whatever you need from me, I am willing."

"Of course, my lady. The vidame insisted that I put my other investigations to the side and focus on your request immediately. He is one of my most vital clients, and I oblige him whenever possible."

"Thank you, sir. You have no idea how important this is to me."

CHAPTER 3

*S*everal weeks had passed since Margaret talked with Mulchere about the search for her brother. She had been told it would not be an easy task since Randall had been presumed dead. In addition, many years had passed since the disappearance, which made tracking down leads even harder, but Mulchere assured her that, if her brother was alive and in France, he would find him. And if he had moved on to another country, he would get that information for her as well.

While Margaret was intently waiting for news, she had tried to keep herself busy with activities around Parintene, such as croquet, riding horses, reading, and spending time with her son. Naturally shy, she was surprised to concede that she was becoming restless being constricted without any external social events. But she still worried that, if she began to engage with the French nobility, it could lead to someone from back home finding out where she was staying. Her priority had to be protecting her son, and if that meant putting her own personal desires aside, she would do it willingly.

As Margaret held her infant son in her arms, she marveled at how he seemed to be changing daily. Henry had been born with only a small sprinkling of curly brown fuzz, but now his hair was beginning to fill in and thicken. And although his hair was dark currently, it could fall out and change into the blond hue of her late husband's in the future. As she stared into her son's beautiful blue eyes, she wondered if they would stay that color. She had heard that most babies were born with blue eyes and that they often changed color as they got older. She hoped that in the next few months she would see his turn into the mesmerizing brown eyes for which the Rolantry family members were known.

But what if they did not change colors? If they stayed blue and his hair stayed brown, she knew it would mean that he did not have any of the Rolantry family features and that he was most likely fathered by... No, she was not going to think about that. It did not matter. He was her son, and she was certain he was going to resemble her late husband once he settled into his looks.

Margaret looked down at her baby boy and laughed softly as she rocked him in her arms. Was that a smile she just saw? She had thought she had seen one at least twice in the past couple of days. Of course, Sarah, her closest servant and dear friend, had told her that it was most likely a reflex on his end. Margaret was determined to believe he was smiling just for her.

Once she heard the soft cooing of sweet slumber, she gently put Henry into his bassinet and sat down to read in the garden.

Mere moments passed by before Margaret heard laughter from the other end of the garden and looked up to see a very small but voluptuous young woman approaching, pulling Pierre by the hand. She had strawberry blonde hair that was artfully arranged atop her head. Margaret noticed as she got closer, the other woman's cheeks were kissed with pink and superbly complemented her smoldering golden-green eyes. Wearing an impeccably tailored jewel-toned green dress and matching jewelry, Margaret recognized the other woman had exquisite taste.

She glanced down at her own loose-fitting brown dress and immediately regretted that she had put little thought into what she was wearing or how she looked. She had not left the estate since arriving in France, causing her to exert little effort into her appearance. She patted her dress, trying to remove some of the wrinkles, and pushed several of her curls into place on top of her head. She had been raised to make a positive first impression, and she did not feel up to the task in her current state.

With the way the young woman was holding Pierre's hand, Margaret wondered with a hint of jealousy if she could be Pierre's love interest. He had told her he was interested in her, but she had shunned his advances. Had he moved on to other pursuits? It should not bother her, because even though Pierre flirted with her and made her acutely aware that he was interested in pursuing her romantically, she was still not ready for a new relationship. In addition, Pierre was not a Christian, and she did not want to form attachments to a man who did not put God as a priority. Logically, she knew all the reasons it should not matter, but the idea of Pierre being with another woman *did* bother her. She did not like it.

When they reached her, Pierre made the introductions. "Countess of Renwick, may I introduce to you the Vicomtesse of Durante, Lady Jacquelyn Seandra Allantes, my cousin and dear friend."

Hesitantly, Margaret looked at Pierre and said with a worried tone, "I thought we agreed that while I was staying with you, you would not be entertaining any visitors."

Pierre laughed off Margaret's disapproval and said, "Jacquelyn is family, and I can guarantee her discretion." He shrugged and chuckled. "Well, at least in regards to your stay at Parintene. I cannot offer assurance in any other matters."

The vicomtesse performed a small curtsy that made her appear bored. The woman grinned while saying, "Although I am pleased to meet you, Lady Margaret, I have to say that I hate formalities and traditions. I figure, if we are to be friends, as Pierre hopes, you should know what you are getting into by accepting me as one. I do, however, enjoy the advantages of having a title."

Jacquelyn winked at her cousin, who was abashed with embarrassment.

"Pardon my cousin, she tends to get... out of hand."

She elbowed him in the side. "You need not make excuses for me, cousin. I am blunt and a handful. All of my lovers will attest to that."

Pierre shook his head in surrender. "They probably would too."

"Oh, do not be such a ninny just because I beat you at cards last night."

"You are a woman, and a lady at that. You should not have been playing cards at that gentlemen's club in the first place."

"Words coming from a poor sport do not count."

The vicomtesse turned back to face Margaret and smiled. "You are going to have so much fun with me, I promise. I am going to teach you things that will make your toes curl, Countess."

Margaret had to laugh. This young woman was the boldest, but most endearing, creature she had ever met. She really liked her, and rarely did she take to someone so fast. She believed it was because she could tell that they were similar in many ways. Neither of them liked the trappings of societal rules, and both treasured their individuality above all else. The vicomtesse was like an outgoing, bubbly version of Margaret.

"I am sure I will, and please, call me Margaret. Pierre does, and I think that I already like you more than him," she teased.

He pouted with fake hurt. "I seem to be the object of *both* your cruelty today. And to think, I actually care for each of you enough to bring you together. Perhaps I should not have. Who knows what will come of it?"

The two women laughed, and the vicomtesse said, "Well, it is too late to undo it now. We have met, and I think Margaret and I are going to become fast friends."

"I have to agree. We are going to get along splendidly."

CHAPTER 4

*M*ulchere continued to search for her brother, and Margaret wanted to help in the endeavor by praying for his return. She also prayed often for her family's future. *God, please help Monsieur Mulchere to find Randall. I feel in my heart that he is still alive. I came to France to find him, and I ask that you guide Monsieur Mulchere's path to locate him. Keep my brother safe until he is returned to us. I also ask that you shield my family and keep us out of harm's way. We need your hedge of protection around us. Help me to trust you and not to worry about what is to come.*

As the time she spent waiting for word from Mulchere lengthened, Margaret recognized her temporary stay in France was turning into a more permanent one. Her plans to relocate to a more remote destination seemed to be indefinitely on hold. After some convincing by Jacquelyn, Margaret decided she should start attending functions in

French society. By paying with cash for everything and using her father's name, Margaret believed it left her undetectable. She had also made sure that neither she nor any of her servants wrote home. It had been part of the condition of them coming with her. By accompanying her, they had chosen to leave all traces of their previous life behind. She had actually been surprised and honored when they chose to follow her to France.

In addition, she knew that if she was going to provide true, lasting security for her son, she was going to have to marry again, and sooner rather than later. That meant she had to begin circulating to find a suitable match, as staying hidden away at Parintene would not help her situation.

She knew she would never love again after losing her husband, but she was also wise enough to know that marriage often had little to do with feelings. She had been lucky once to be able to say she had truly loved her husband; she was not impractical enough to think it would happen twice. However, it did not mean she would compromise on her requirements, and she needed her future husband to be a Christian above all else. It was the one glaring reason she could not allow Pierre to court her, as he did not care to pursue religion.

After she gave the go-ahead for Jacquelyn to start planning her social calendar, Margaret found herself being constantly pulled from one function to the next by the cousins. Her life in France was such a strong contrast to her life in England. Living in the center of Paris was so different than how she lived in her country home. There was little opportunity to meet new people, as most celebrations, get-togethers, and balls consisted of the same people who lived nearby. But the city was a bustling, lively entity all its own, filled with magical operas, decadent cafés, and glorious masquerades. In addition, she was being introduced to all sorts of new types of people, from actors, to artists, to musicians, and her eyes were being opened to all varieties of life.

All of French society was dazzled by the beauty from across the sea, and everywhere Margaret went, people flocked to her side. In England, she would have been reluctant to allow herself to be the center of attention, but somehow, Jacquelyn made her enjoy it when they were together. And they were always together, as they had become inseparable.

She was beginning to appreciate living in France and found that she did not miss England as much as she had in the beginning. She was even starting to realize that, just because her first choice of living a quiet life in the country had been taken from her, this new life, with her different friends, was equally wonderful in its own way.

But deep in her heart, she could feel that, even though her life in France was full of new and thrilling experiences, she was missing something by not giving God his equal portion of her attention. She prayed every night and read her Bible every morning, but since being in France, she had not taken the time to find a church to attend. Part of it was due to not knowing Paris, but deep down she knew that if she truly wanted to, she could have asked Pierre and he would be able to tell her of any number of nearby churches. The real issue was that she did not think her new friends would appreciate her religious needs, and because of that, she had decided to keep her faith to herself.

She knew she was not doing right by herself or her father, whose dying wish was for her to have a relationship with God, yet she could not bring herself to broach the subject with either Pierre or Jacquelyn. She just kept hoping the situation would work itself out.

Margaret had just returned from an evening out at the theatre where they watched the latest performance by the playwright Simon Shaw. He also happened to be one of Jacquelyn's many admirers. She had an ever-rotating list. It had been an interesting play, but she found her friend's interaction with Simon even more entertaining when Jacquelyn caught him kissing another woman backstage.

Jacquelyn was a spitfire, and she marched right up to Simon and smacked him soundly across the face. "I play second to no one, least of all to a third-row chorus girl who does not have the common sense to see an impecunious dramatist for who he is."

Everyone around them was shocked by her behavior, except Margaret and Pierre. They were accustomed to her shenanigans. Margaret had to pull Jacquelyn away from the shouting match, and it took several hours for Jacquelyn to calm down after. What had started out as a pleasant enough night had turned into a tediously long one.

Margaret yawned as she made her way towards her dressing room. She knew Motty and Francisca should be on their way to help her undress for the evening, so she sat down at her vanity to unpin her hair. As she was removing the last of the pins, Sarah entered the room with a worried look on her face.

It was surprising to see Sarah, as she was supposed to be in the nursery with Henry. Since Margaret had the baby, Sarah had unofficially taken on the role as his nanny. These days, it was rare to see Sarah without Henry in her arms.

"Something is amiss. What is it?" Margaret asked.

"Yes, my lady. As you know, he hasn't been feeling well the past few days and has been fussy with a slight fever. We all assumed it was because he was getting his first tooth, but this evening, the fever has increased significantly and his condition has worsened."

"What do you mean, 'his condition has worsened'?"

"I think you should come with me, my lady."

Jumping up from her chair, Margaret hurriedly followed Sarah out of her bedroom chambers, rushing down the hall to Henry's nursery. The room was illuminated with a few candles, and Motty was sitting in the rocking chair with a limp Henry on her lap.

Margaret could tell immediately that something was drastically wrong. It was apparent that Motty had been crying, as her eyes were red and puffy and there were tearstains on her cheeks. Henry lay flaccid and was an odd shade of pale with black circles under his eyes. He did not look well at all. Margaret's stomach tightened in terror, and she forced herself to swallow the lump in the back of her throat.

"Please, hand me my son."

Motty stood up and swiftly handed Henry over to Margaret. "I am so sorry, my lady. We had no idea he would get this sick so suddenly."

"Leave me alone with him and send for the doctor directly. Make sure he is aware that it is urgent."

Afraid she might faint from fear, Margaret walked over to the chair and sat down. She could sense whatever ailed her son was severe. He was exceedingly hot to the touch and had a heavy line of sweat along his curly brown hair. It felt as if she were touching a live flame as she gently placed her hand on his forehead. He was struggling for every breath and she could hear a slight wheezing underneath.

As she looked down at her son, he appeared so small in her arms. It did not seem fair to have him lying there so incredibly ill. She had barely gotten any time with him. If he did not pull through what ailed him, he would never get the chance to grow up. He would never crawl or walk or speak. She would never hear him say he loved her. He would never wrap his arms around her and kiss her cheek good night. He would never go to school, fall in love, or get married. The idea of losing so much time with him made Margaret shake with fright.

Tears cascaded down her face as she clutched Henry to her chest. What started out as soft cries turned into full-body sobs she could not control. What would she do if she lost him? She had already lost her father and husband, and she did not know if she was going to find her brother. Her son was all the family she had left and the most important thing in her life. She did not think she could survive his loss. Mothers were not meant to bury a child.

Margaret knew Henry's life was in God's hands. She trusted God, so she knew she had to pray. Shakily, she stood up and placed her son's frail body on the chair, then fell to her knees beside him. *Lord, I know you gave me Henry for a reason. Please, Lord, do not take him from me. I will do anything you ask of me. I am so scared. I cannot make it through this without your strength. Your word says that when I am weak, you are strong, so please give me your strength. I cannot get through this without you. Please, God, heal my son. I beg you, save him!*

As Margaret waited for the doctor to arrive, a poem she read in a book that was read to a dying child came to mind. She repeated it out loud, believing every word.

"Jesus loves me—this I know
For the Bible tells me so
Little ones to him belong,
They are weak, but he is strong.

"Jesus loves me—loves me still,
Though I am very weak and ill;
From his shining throne on high

Comes to watch me where I lie.

"Jesus loves me—he will stay
Close beside me all the way.
Then his little child will take
Up to Heaven for his dear sake."

She wondered how anyone was able to surrender a child to the Lord. She wished she had the fortitude to have the peace to do the same, but selfishly, she wanted her son to stay with her.

The doctor arrived at the vidame's estate after two hours' time. As the elderly, grey-haired man entered the nursery, he adjusted his glasses upon his long nose and walked over to Margaret.

"I have been informed that something seems to be wrong with your little one, Countess."

"Yes, Doctor Labonte. I am distraught with concern."

"Can you bring him over to the changing table so that I may examine him?"

Margaret did as requested, placing him on the table and anxiously watching as the doctor touched the boy's body, listened with a stethoscope to his chest, and lifted his eyelids to check his pupils, all the while saying nothing.

After thoroughly checking the baby, he turned to Margaret. "Your son has pneumonia."

She inhaled sharply and shook her head in denial. "No, that is not possible. He was perfectly satisfactory a couple of days ago, but then he started teething. You must be mistaken."

"I should clarify, my lady. Your son has pneumonia, but extraordinarily, his fever seems to be reducing moment by moment. This never happens, especially in ones so young. It almost always turns out the child does not survive." The doctor reached out and touched the child's forehead and rubbed his grey beard with his other hand. "Every time I touch him, he is cooler. When a child has pneumonia, that does not happen. I am baffled by what I am witnessing."

"Truly? You mean my son is healed?"

"I would not say that yet, but I do believe he is on his way to being so. We will need to keep an eye on him, and I will be stopping by daily to determine that he is still on the mend. If he continues to get better and does not relapse by week's end, your son should be cured."

"I believe in God, Doctor Labonte, and I prayed for my son's recovery earlier this evening. He was still horribly sick at the time, and I feared the worst. But God has decided to give me a miracle. I know it, without a shadow of a doubt."

"I am also a believer, Countess, and I have only seen a handful of true miracles in my forty years in medicine."

"This is my first one."

Margaret picked up her son and kissed the top of his head. God saved her son, and she knew she would never forget it.

CHAPTER 5

Two weeks had passed since Henry had fallen ill and he was completely recovered. Margaret did not leave his side for the first several days, but Pierre and Jacquelyn insisted that it was time for her to resume social activities again. For her first outing, the cousins were taking her out to a café on the Boulevard des Italiens.

Taking one last look in her vanity mirror, Margaret adjusted her crinoline domed skirt and nodded in approval, noting that the deep purple of her dress enhanced her eyes perfectly. She grabbed her belongings for the evening and headed out the door.

The carriage ride to the Café Anglais was uneventful as Margaret's mind was churning with anticipation of the exciting night that lay ahead. It was an exceptionally hard place to gain entry in order to enjoy a meal, but luckily,

Pierre had all the right connections to get them in anywhere they chose.

The Café Anglais was ornate in its bright white and golden décor. With gold leaf patina mirrors and mahogany and walnut wood furnishings, the ambience was elegant and stately.

The servers were bustling back and forth and weaving in and out from the crowds, the café overflowing with patrons.

Jacquelyn could not stop talking about the renowned chef Adolphe Dugléré, who was cooking for their party tonight. Apparently, he was one of the most illustrious chefs in all of Paris and known for his delectable French cuisine. He had studied under Marie-Antoine Carême, who taught him in the style of haute cuisine, the "high art" of French cooking.

Margaret and Jacquelyn made their way into one of the dining salons while Pierre gave the carriage driver instructions for returning after the party was over.

"We are going to have such a great time, Margaret. I hear that Adolphe has planned an eleven-course menu just for us and it is filled with decadence. Pierre also told me that he has even arranged for Adolphe to come have a drink with us at the end of the meal."

"It sounds lovely, Jackie," Margaret said, using the nickname the vicomtesse insisted her friends and family called her.

Looking around the room, Margaret noted that there was a diverse crowd with them, including a few actors and actresses from the nearby legendary Salle Le Peletier, two famous artists, a novelist, and several aristocrats.

Pierre arrived and helped Margaret into her seat while saying, "Are you ready to have your taste buds tantalized, Margaret?"

"You indulge us extravagantly, Pierre."

"I would not have it any other way." Pierre took his seat across from Margaret while Jackie sat down next to her. Immediately, her friend was engaged in conversation by one of the actors sitting on Jacquelyn's other side.

Margaret watched as their glasses were filled with white Bordeaux wine, and the first hors d'oeuvre course was served in union. She began to eat the canapes a l'amiral when a well-dressed man sat in the other seat next to her.

He addressed the table in a leisurely manner, "Pardon my interruption, ladies and gentlemen. I was unable to... detangle myself from a previous engagement."

Several of the other guests began to laugh, knowing he must have just returned from a dalliance with someone. A couple of the women at the table whispered while demurely eyeing the stranger.

Curiously, Margaret glanced over at him. Who was he that he could cause such a flurry of interest? He was striking in an unusual way with his curly black hair, which he left natural and hung just down past the nape of his neck. He had pale green eyes and expressive, bold eyebrows. As she watched him, he began to smile and she realized that was what drew all the women to him. He had dimples on both cheeks that made his smile irresistible.

Leaning over to Jackie, Margaret whispered, "Who is the man sitting next to me?"

Jackie grinned knowingly. "That is Eduard Voclain, one of the most gossiped about artists in all of Paris. His reputation is quite provocative, as it is rumored that, if he paints a woman, she must pay him first in ways other than money."

The soup course arrived and Margaret silently said a prayer over her food, then mechanically started eating as she thought about Jackie's words. What would it be like to be painted by a man like that? The only portrait she had ever done was when she lived in England and her father had commissioned one in honor of her fourteenth birthday. The painter had been an old crotchety man who snapped at her constantly, making her nervous the entire time. She suspected Eduard Voclain would make her nervous as well, but for an entirely different reason.

"You do not seem to be enjoying your soup."

Margaret looked over at Eduard and replied, "Whatever gave you that impression?"

"You are not smiling, and that is a shame because I am betting you have a remarkable smile. What would it take for me to put a smile on that stunning face of yours?"

Oh goodness, he was a smooth one. She reddened at the blatant flirting.

"How charming. You are so fresh you can still blush. I wonder where else I could make you blush."

He *was* right. Even though it had been going on since she started circulating in French society, she still had not gotten used to all the ceaseless innuendos.

"Do you talk in such a way to all women to whom you have not even been properly introduced?"

He winked at her. "I do not have to know your name to know I want to get to know you. But if it makes you feel more comfortable to know my name, I am Eduard Voclain."

She retorted indignantly, "I never said I wanted to know your name."

He leaned back in his chair and whistled lightly. "My, my, you are a fiery one. I am liking you more and more all the time, Miss…." He waited for her to fill in the blank.

Reluctantly, she replied in a chiding tone, "*Lady* Margaret, Countess of Renwick."

In a slightly mocking but amusing way, Eduard asked, "I was wondering, Lady Margaret, Countess of Renwick, would you be interested in letting me paint your portrait sometime?"

Margaret had to admit that he was rather formidable when he was determined to get what he wanted. She had thought that by her curt replies, he would realize she was not interested in a dalliance. Yet she had to admit to herself that he was amusing her. Would it hurt if she continued to let him flirt? What's more, if she flirted back?

"What exactly would me letting you paint me entail, Monsieur Voclain?"

"Please, call me Eduard." He leaned in towards her, whispering in her ear so only she could hear, his breath brushing across her cheek suggestively. "You would come over to my studio and I would pour you a glass of wine. You would make yourself comfortable, anywhere you like, and I would begin to ever so slowly make long, deliberate strokes, ending with"—Margaret squeezed her lips together and clenched her hands in her lap. Her heart beat wildly in her chest as she imagined what he described. He finished with a flippant tone —"a picture of you on canvas, of course."

She let out the air she had been holding in and laughed. "I have to say, Eduard, you have a way with words."

"That is not the only thing with which I have a way."

Pierre, obviously overhearing their exchange, interjected, "Monsieur Voclain, I would appreciate you being respectable when you speak to Lady Margaret."

Eduard shifted his gaze over to Pierre and asked nonchalantly, "What is it of your concern how I talk to her?"

"Let me rephrase. I think it best if you discontinue talking to her altogether. Lady Margaret does not need to be bothered by someone like you."

Everyone around the table stopped talking and watched the confrontation between the two men.

"You do not even know me, so why would you think you have the right to comment on my character? Besides, Margaret does not seem to be complaining."

"You imbecile, how dare you address her so informally."

Shocked, Margaret covered her gaping mouth with her gloved hand. This happened every time a man showed any interest in her. She did not need him getting involved in her interactions all the time.

"Pierre, what has gotten into you? May I please speak with you privately?"

With a frown on his face, Pierre nodded in agreement. He came around to her side of the table, firmly grabbed her by the arm, and escorted her out into the hallway. Once away from prying ears, Margaret scolded, "What were you thinking, Pierre? The way you acted in there, people are going to think something is going on between us."

Pierre looked at Margaret longingly. "Would that be so bad, Margaret? What if I told you I want there to be something going on between us?"

"But there cannot be. It would not work. *We* would not work."

He stepped closer to her and affectionately said, "Why can it not work? I think we could be surprising together."

She shook her head. "No, Pierre, you need to stop behaving like this. I am not yours."

Seeming frustrated with her denial of their connection, Pierre pulled her into his arms. "That remains to be seen. In the meantime, I am going to show you there *is* something going on between us." And with that, he dipped his head down and placed his lips upon hers.

Margaret had been afraid that she would never be able to respond with desire again. She had purposefully avoided physical contact with men because the last time someone kissed her, it had been violent. Part of her was afraid she would never be able to stomach a man's touch again. She was wrong. The kiss was searing and made her quiver in all the right ways.

She knew she should not be letting him do it because he was right about one thing—there was something going on between them. She had to stop it before it went any further. She pulled free from the kiss and pushed against his chest, saying resolutely, "That was a mistake."

"It was not a mistake, Margaret. It was inevitable. *We* are inevitable."

"You are wrong. I have to go. I cannot stay here any longer."

Margaret turned away and hurried out of the café. The rush of cold air blew across her face as she found herself on the street. She realized that Pierre had sent their carriage away and it would be hours before it was back. It did not matter; she could walk to Parintene. She needed the time to clear her head anyway.

Disturbed by their physical encounter, she knew why they would not work. She needed a Christian husband, and she knew Pierre had no room for God in his life. She had made the mistake of falling for the wrong man before because of foolish desires; she was not about to do it again, no matter how strong the enticement.

She thought about their misguided kiss and knew Pierre was the worst kind of temptation. His touch was like a lit match that set her on fire. Every inch of her tingled with yearning, and she desperately wanted to turn around and run back into his arms. She knew she could not give in to it, because if she did, there would be no turning back.

Suddenly, she felt someone grab her from around the waist while a hand roughly covered her mouth. Margaret tried to scream, but it was muffled against the gloved hand that was pushed against her delicate skin.

"Be still, girl, and this will all be over quick," said a gruff voice with a thick Irish accent.

The mugger was pulling her backwards into an alleyway where the darkness would cover all traces of them. Trepidation filled her as flashes of the duke's attack came crashing back. Her body shuddered with terror as horrifying memories pushed in on her. Trying to calm herself so she could find a way out of her perilous predicament, Margaret forced herself to focus on what was going on right now, not what had happened to her in the past. What did *this* man want? She hoped it was only money.

"I am going to take my hand off your mouth, but if you scream, you're going to regret it. Do you understand, missy?"

She vehemently nodded in agreement.

He removed his hand from her mouth, but before she could ask him what he wanted, he used his free hand to touch her body. She whimpered in protest but did not scream.

"Good girl. You stay still just like that."

"What do you want?" Margaret asked in a whisper.

"My first inkling was whatever valuables you have, but

after what I just felt, I think I may be taking some of your other goods as well."

"Please, please, sir, my family is wealthy. I can get you whatever you want. Just let me go!"

"Ah, a noble lady. I don't think I've ever had the pleasure."

Margaret started to squirm, trying to break free. "I know people, important people who will have your hide if you hurt me."

"They're not here now, are they? You'd be smart not to make threats against me. But you can keep on struggling. I kinda like that."

She froze, not wanting to make matters worse. She could not go through this type of assault again. The last time nearly killed her. She would not survive it a second time. What was she going to do?

Pray. It was all she could do. *Please, God, please help me! I am so scared. I do not know what to do. I need you, Lord. Please, please send someone to help me!*

From the edge of the street, she saw an approaching figure rush up to them, yelling, "Get your hands off the lady."

Thank you, Lord. Thank you for hearing my prayers.

"Monsieur, you best be leaving. This isn't any of your concern."

"I think it is you who ought to be leaving before I yell for the police. I saw one just a moment ago."

A look of fear crossed the mugger's face before he said in insolence, "I bet you're bluffing."

"Am I? I would not take that bet if I were you."

Margaret felt the hesitation in the man's body; he waivered and then let her go.

"You're one lucky girl." The mugger took off down the alley and was gone within seconds.

She was shaking uncontrollably and leaned against the wall of the nearby building for support. A queasiness had formed in the pit of her stomach, and she felt like she might be sick. She crossed her arms around her body and whispered to the stranger who saved her, "Thank you, sir, for intervening."

It was still dark where they were standing, and she could not make out any of the stranger's features. "It was nothing. Anyone would have done the same."

Margaret shook her head in protest. "No, not everyone. You saved my life."

"What are you doing all alone out here? This is no place for a lady."

"I got into a fight with a friend, and I left the dinner party we were attending. I am new to Paris and must have gotten lost. I am afraid I do not know where I am."

"Can I be of assistance?"

"If you can point me in the right direction, I would greatly appreciate it."

The cold was setting in and she shuddered. Noticing it, the stranger said, "Here, take my coat. You will catch your death with only that shawl around you."

He placed the coat over her shoulders and gently guided her towards the street.

"My carriage is just around the corner. I had just finished negotiating some antiques at the store at the corner when I heard something from the alley. At first, I thought it was a rat, but something made me look into it further."

Margaret knew it had been God. She prayed He would send someone and He did.

"I am grateful you followed your instincts."

As they approached the streetlight, Margaret looked at the man who had rescued her. From his attire, he appeared to be wealthy, wearing a fitted charcoal grey suit and matching vest. He was pleasant-looking, but not in the traditional sense. His features leaned towards interesting instead of attractive with olive-colored skin, a long angular nose, and a distinct jawline. He wore his dark brown hair parted on the right side, which framed his deep grey eyes and thick eyebrows. Some would even say the gentleman was handsome, in a foreign sort of way.

"This is my carriage. May I take you home?"

She hesitated for a moment, apprehensive of getting into a carriage with a stranger. He reached out his hand to her, but she did not take it.

"How ill-mannered of me. I should introduce myself. I am Lord Michel Robineau, the Marquis de Badour."

Smiling at him, Margaret accepted his hand. "Under the circumstances, it is not your fault that we have not been properly introduced."

"You have not given me your name."

"Lady Margaret Wellesley, Countess of Renwick."

"I really do think we should be getting you back to your residence. Where did you say you lived?"

But before she could answer the marquis, she heard Jackie say from behind, "There you are, Margaret. What are you doing all the way over here? We were looking everywhere for you. We were so worried."

Margaret turned around to find Pierre and Jackie looking at them through their carriage window.

Taking in her disheveled appearance, Pierre asked, "What happened?"

"I will explain later. Can you please take me home?"

"Yes, of course, straightaway."

Both Pierre and Jackie looked at the marquis in puzzlement but said nothing. As Margaret got into the carriage, she said to her rescuer, "Thank you again, my lord."

"Good night, Lady Margaret."

CHAPTER 6

*M*argaret had watched all night as everyone around the marquis, many of whom she had previously met and knew to be titled and wealthy, fawned all over him and waited on his every word. She knew he had to be exceptionally powerful to elicit that type of attention. What surprised her was that he did not seem to be affected by it. It was almost as if he was not aware of his own influence on people.

She liked that. It was a sharp contrast to the duke, who had reveled in his title and wealth and made sure to lord it over everyone. Even her own Henry had used his status to control others. It was one of the few flaws that had displeased her about her late husband.

Margaret noted that beyond the obvious effect the marquis had on those around him, due to his prominence, he was also fashionable without being garish, wearing a black suit with a complementing vest and bow tie. But the most impressive part about him was that he did not present as being vain.

Next to him sat a younger man who was much more conspicuous in both dress and appearance. His attire was significantly flashier, and it was clear he wanted to be noticed. It was also obvious he was related to the man next to him, as their physical attributes were similar. The younger man seemed to enjoy the attention that the marquis brought to their opera box. The marquis had one of the best boxes in the theater, affording him and his guests privacy due to the enclosed sides, as well as a spectacular view from the front.

The young man flirted with the many women, married as well as unwed, who came through to introduce themselves. The marquis, on the other hand, although polite to everyone, did not demonstrate an interest in any of the women.

This made Margaret wonder about the availability of the marquis. Was he already spoken for, or did his tastes lie elsewhere? He acutely intrigued her ever since he'd rescued her two nights before. She found her thoughts drifting back to him and how he had made her feel safe when he took care of her during the attempted mugging. He was a curious combination of sincere and steadfast, and for the first time, she found herself contemplating the real possibility of finding a husband in France. The one question that remained was whether or not he was a Christian. She would have to inconspicuously do some digging to find out.

Lost in contemplation, Margaret did not realize that she

had been blatantly staring at their box. The younger man looked over and gave a smug smile. Did he mistakenly think she was interested in him? Margaret blushed, embarrassed to be caught watching someone.

She averted her eyes and gathered her possessions. Abruptly, she stood up, ready to make a bolt for the exit.

Jackie looked over at Margaret, startled by her friend's sudden movements. "What is going on, chéri?"

Glancing coyly at the box next to them, Margaret let out a sigh of relief. Both men were absent, most likely having left to go home since the opera had ended. She sat down and pulled out her fan from her clutch. She was flush from mortification and reflexively flicked her fan back and forth near her face.

Not happy with being ignored, Jackie elbowed the countess and asked again, with clear irritation in her voice, "You are making a scene, which is unlike you. What seems to be the predicament?"

Margaret whispered back, "I will tell you later, but I think it is time to leave, Jackie."

"Sometimes you are so odd. I honestly do not know why I put up with you."

Concerned with getting away without bumping into their neighbors, Margaret chose to disregard her friend's comment. Besides, considering all the antics that Jackie pulled, she figured her breach in etiquette was far less humiliating than what Jackie did on a regular basis.

The two women got up from their seats and started to

exit their opera box, but unexpectedly their path was blocked.

Margaret stiffened, holding her breath. Despite trying to mask her shock, her eyes grew round with astonishment. She regrettably recognized the arrogant owner of the smug smile staring back at her.

The young man moved forward into their box, forcing the women to quickly take several steps back.

"May I introduce myself? I am Lord Monte Robineau, brother to the Marquis de Badour."

Jackie tilted her head to the side and stared at the man with a confused look on her face. Monte glanced from Jackie to Margaret with amusement. "I assumed from your companion's apparent interest in our box that a proper introduction was in order. To satiate her curiosity, of course."

Jerking her attention to the side, Jackie gave her friend a perplexed look.

Margaret lifted her chin in bravado. "I have not the faintest idea what you are referring to, sir."

He laughed, shaking his head. "Come now, it was quite clear you were taken with me. I thought the least I could do was come over here and make your imaginings come to life by letting you meet me."

Narrowing her eyes in annoyance, Margaret said candidly, "I am not interested in *you* whatsoever."

After a moment's hesitation, he raised both eyebrows and nodded in realization. "So, it is the marquis who piqued your interest? Will surprises never cease? I suppose you will be wanting an introduction to him, then. I could make—"

Margaret cut him off. "That will not be necessary. You are mistaken... again."

Apparently, Monte did not know that she had already made his brother's acquaintance. Margaret pushed past him without making any eye contact.

She could hear Jackie behind her. "Pardon the countess. She is not feeling herself. We need to be going, but I hope we might have a chance to get better acquainted another time."

"My, my, I did not see this on the horizon but find myself contemplating the possibilities."

At Margaret's quickened pace, she found herself out of hearing within seconds. Deciding she needed a moment to pull herself together, she headed for the powder room. She could not believe that he had the gall to come over and confront her. Although, from what she could make of the man, she could tell he liked keeping people off balance. She did not like *that* at all.

As she rounded the next corner in a rush, she accidently bumped into someone. Her clutch and fan tumbled from her hands onto the floor. Quickly, she bent down to gather her items, and after a few moments, noticed that there was a second set of hands helping her. She glanced up and froze in place.

This night could not get any worse. Of all the people to crash into, it had to be the Marquis de Badour. She could only hope that his brother had not told him that she had been staring at their box earlier.

"Excuse me, Lady Margaret. I did not see you coming around the corner."

She tried to maintain an even voice while replying, "No, pardon me, my lord. It was my fault. I was not paying sufficient attention to where I was going."

As they stood up, he seemed to be studying her. She had no idea what he was thinking, and she found it unnerving. Wanting to quickly get out of his presence, she said, "Thank you for your assistance. It was most appreciated."

She moved past the marquis but stopped in her tracks when she heard him say, "Must you hurry off? I was hoping to elicit a few moments of your time."

She turned around and stared at the man who had transfixed her thoughts the past couple of days. "What would you like to converse with me regarding, my lord?"

"I have to say, I am glad I elected to come tonight. I had almost decided against it. I think that would have been a mistake."

Relaxing a bit, Margaret allowed herself to smile, realizing that she was glad he had come as well. "Are you not an admirer of the opera?"

"If I am honest, I am not the most social of people. I find the majority of these events to be most tedious." He looked intently at her, adding, "Although, at the moment, I find myself becoming more and more an admirer of the opera."

She returned his look with ease. "I am pleased you came

this evening. I wanted to thank you again for the other night. If you had not arrived when you did, I am not sure what would have happened to me."

"Lady Margaret, let us never speak of it again. The only good to come of it was, at least, I was able to meet you. I was wondering if I would be able to—"

Unexpectedly, Margaret felt a hand grip the bottom of her elbow. She turned her head to find Pierre standing next to her. "There you are, Margaret. I was finally able to get the matter resolved that took me away earlier this evening."

With all that had happened, Margaret had completely forgotten that Pierre had left in the middle of the opera due to some business concerns.

"Pierre, I am surprised you came back, considering the opera already ended."

Pointedly he looked at the Marquis. "*I* wanted to make sure you had an escort home, as I imagined my cousin might end up leaving you on your own." He looked around and a scowl crossed his face. "It seems I was right to be concerned, as I do not see Jackie anywhere."

"She was right behind me, Pierre. She was only momentarily delayed." Margaret gently pulled her elbow free and stepped away. "I am grateful for your thoughtfulness, but I am capable of finding my own way home."

"On the contrary, the other night, when you were accosted, should prove that you are not safe on your own."

"Pierre, that was an isolated incident. I have been to the opera multiple times and know my way back to Parintene readily. I think it best if you allow me to take care of myself." She was not finished with her conversation with the marquis, which had been cut off when Pierre interrupted. She most keenly wanted to know what he wanted to ask her. "I have some matters I wish to attend to before I am ready to leave."

Immediately, she saw the wounded look in Pierre's eyes and internally cringed as she did not want to hurt her friend. However, she knew that Pierre had been consistently becoming more possessive over her, and she could not have him running off every eligible suitor who pursued her.

"I can make sure the countess arrives home safely." Margaret turned to look at the marquis, shocked that he would get involved in what might appear to be a lover's quarrel.

"Thank you, Lord Robineau." She turned back to Pierre and stated with certainty, "You are free to go, Pierre."

Pierre was visibly furious. He paused for a moment, and Margaret could tell by his frustrated posture that he wanted to object. Instead, he nodded in acceptance and said, "If you will excuse me, I will be on my way, then."

Swiftly, Pierre turned back around and walked towards the exit of the opera house.

After several seconds, Margaret returned her attention to the marquis. "I hope that did not give you the wrong impression. He is only a family friend, and as I am currently staying as a guest at his estate, he seems to feel the need to be protective."

The marquis raised a hand and shook his head indifferently. "No need to explain. It was none of my concern, but it did seem that you were uncomfortable with his conduct, and that is why I stepped in by offering to escort you home."

"Escort me home? You said you would make sure I arrived home safely. I assumed you meant that you would make sure I safely returned in a carriage." Not wanting to create difficulty for the marquis, she concluded, "I would not want to inconvenience you in any way."

The marquis reached out and took her arm. "When I say I am going to do something, I do it. I take my word very seriously." Softening his tone, he added, "Besides, I want to escort you home. I find myself looking for any excuse to spend more time with you."

"Before we depart, I need to find my friend and let her know I will be leaving for the evening."

"As you wish, my lady. I can accompany you while you search for her."

A few moments later, Margaret found Jackie talking with Monte in a secluded corner near their opera boxes. As she approached them, Margaret could tell by her friend's mannerism, she was flirting with Monte.

"There you are, mon chéri. I had wondered where you had gone."

"I can see you are occupied at the moment. The Marquis de Badour has graciously offered to escort me to Parintene. Do you wish to come with us?"

Jackie gave Margaret a knowing smile. "Thank you for the invitation, but I think I shall stay a while longer."

Monte interjected, "I will make sure the vicomtesse arrives home safely." He winked at his brother, and added, "You need not wait up for me, brother. I have no plans to be home any time soon."

Reluctant to allow Jackie to remain in Monte's questionable company, Margaret warned, "Do be careful, Jackie. I would not want anything to happen to you."

Jackie nodded. "I appreciate your concern. I believe I am in capable hands."

After saying good night, Margaret and the marquis made their way to the theater exit. Several heads turned towards them and watched as they departed. By night's end, the gossip circles would have a new piece of fodder. She knew it would not be long before everyone was asking her about her time with him.

As they rode along in the marquis's carriage, she could tell that he seemed a bit apprehensive around her. She was not sure why he was uneasy in her presence, but it made her wonder.

"Pardon me, my lord, but is something bothering you?"

He looked at her thoughtfully and waited several moments before replying. "It is not that anything is the matter. It is more that I find myself fascinated by you in a way I have never been with a woman."

Oh, so that was it. She had thought that perhaps he had changed his mind about getting to know her but did not know how to broach the subject. She had no idea that it was just the opposite. He felt uncomfortable around her *because* he wanted to get to know her far better than he cared to acknowledge.

"I would think you have spent a great deal of time around many women more fascinating than I."

"On the contrary, you seem to be substantiated, poised, and deeply conscientious. Rare traits in the noble women with whom I have been acquainted."

She glanced away while saying, "I appreciate the flattery, but I think you do me more justice than I deserve."

He smiled. "Did I forget to include humble? That is a quality I have not found in a woman since my mother."

Margaret blushed at the adoration she could hear in the marquis's voice. She did not expect to have him praise her in this fashion. She had to admit, it felt wonderful to have him do so. *But,* she reminded herself, *he does not know about your son or your past. It can, and most likely will, change how he feels about you once he does.*

Saddened by the thought that as quickly as the marquis's admiration could be given to her, it could be taken away by her past, Margaret gathered her things together to depart in a hurry.

As the carriage pulled up to Parintene, she averted her eyes from the marquis. She did not want him to see her shame as she thought about her past. She hated that what had been done to her by a hateful monster would possibly keep her from ever finding happiness again. It seemed so unfair.

In a detached tone, Margaret said, "Thank you for escorting me home, my lord." When she placed her hand on the door handle of the carriage to open it, the marquis rested his own over hers to stop her from leaving.

Confused, he asked, "It seems now something is bothering you. What has changed so suddenly?"

"Nothing. I just momentarily forgot that I have obligations, and I think once you are aware of them, you may become disinterested in me. I cannot afford to let myself be imprudent."

He shook his head and gently pulled her hands into his own.

"If you are referring to your situation, I am aware that you are a widow and have a son. It does not change anything on my end."

Margaret was surprised by the blunt statement. Curiosity made her ask, "How do you know this about me?"

"I must confess, after our chance encounter the other night, I made some inquiries. You interested me, and I wanted to know more about you. I had planned to introduce myself earlier tonight but had not found the right time to do so. Bumping into you after the performance was a perfectly timed accident."

Margaret began to laugh softly. "We seem to experience those often."

"You find this amusing?"

"Not so much what you did, but the fact that I had left my seat tonight in a hurry because your brother caught me staring at you."

She had no idea why she confessed that embarrassing bit of truth. She did not have to, and she realized it gave him the upper hand by doing so. Why was it that this man was able to get her to disclose things she did not plan on confessing?

"I have to profess, I am pleased that this is not one-sided."

"It is not, I assure you."

"Then I hope that this is not too forward, but if you will be in attendance at church tomorrow, I would like to sit with you."

"I have not found a church as of yet, but I would not be opposed to attend the one to which you go."

"I attend at Taitbout Chapel. May I collect you tomorrow morning on my way to the service?"

Margaret nodded in agreement. "I would be pleased."

CHAPTER 7

*S*tanding outside the chapel, Margaret was grateful that her questions about the marquis's religious preference had been answered. It seemed that if their relationship progressed towards marriage, she would finally be able to be with a husband who was as committed to God as she had become. It was refreshing to not worry that her desire to grow in the Lord would not be met with disapproval or mockery but instead with like-mindedness.

She had not been able to attend church for several months, and as she walked through the doors, she felt an overwhelming peace wash over her.

As they walked to their seats towards the front of the chapel, several parishioners welcomed them with smiles and warm greetings. The marquis did not stop to converse, most likely to keep her from being overwhelmed.

After several hymns were sung by the congregation, the pastor, Eugène Bersier, came to the front and took his place behind the pulpit.

"Welcome, dear brothers and sisters. We have been talking about the attributes of love over the past several weeks. I feel that we still have so much to examine when it comes to this subject. True love requests a duality of the most distinct individuality of a person coupled with the most intimate association with one another. This love, which is given to us only through the grace of God, is the source of all that is important. It grounds us in conviction, in truth, in certainty, and in joy. Jesus Christ, through his death on the cross and subsequent resurrection, opened access to an all-powerful love that is capable of doing wondrous acts in and around us. It has the power to free us from sin, to turn the lost towards purpose, and to usher us into eternal life. The Holy Bible states that we are to love one another because everyone who loves is born of God and knows God. Therefore, it is our duty to love each other as God loves us. Let us bow our heads to pray for God to show us the way to love one another according to His will."

Margaret could not believe that, after being unable to attend church for so long, the message was about love upon her return. Her father's pastor, Reverend Fisher, had changed her life back in England and helped her find salvation through a message about love, and now, as she sat next to a man she hoped to one day marry, she was hearing another sermon about love in the most profound new context.

According to Pastor Eugène Bersier not only was being an individual acceptable but it was also needed to best serve the Lord. That meant that all of the obstacles, setbacks, and losses that she went through in her life were not a hindrance but a blessing. She could use them to help others, and if she allowed God to work in her, He would use those past pains to change her for the better.

In addition, she was beginning to understand that God chose to design her with her unique quirks and imperfections. They were not flaws but rather instruments He would use to show God's love. There was freedom in that, knowing that she did not have to live up to expectations she or others placed on her. The only one she needed to please was God, and He loved her just the way He made her.

Margaret had been reading as she sat on the bench by the window when Pierre came into the room to inform her that Mulchere had returned with an urgent matter to discuss with her.

She stood as the detective came into the room with a sullen look on his face. Reflexively, she asked with dread, "Does this concern my brother? Are you here to tell me Randall is dead?"

Rapidly blinking several times in confusion, he replied,

"No, this has nothing to do with your brother. I have something else that I need to tell you. It is of the upmost importance."

Worried, Margaret asked with slight impatience, "What is it?"

"While I was searching for information regarding your brother, I came across some people who were looking for you, Lady Margaret. I only tell you this because they had British accents and they were… forceful in their hunt."

Her face became tight with worry and she pursed her lips. This was bad. That meant that someone from home was trying to track her down. She had been stupid not to realize that by using her father's title, even in a foreign country, it would eventually lead someone straight to her if they were looking.

"Can you find out for whom these people are working?"

"It was evident that the men I encountered were hired mercenaries. I asked around as to whom they had been employed by, but I could not get any details. Whoever dispatched them seems to be well funded, as they were diligent and efficient at their investigative tasks. They were starting their search in the lesser-known areas, I think, because they assumed you were in hiding. They are currently unaware that you are cosseted amongst the French titled."

This changed everything. It would be only a matter of weeks, possibly days, before whoever sent the mercenaries found her. She had to come up with a plan to throw them off her trail while Mulchere continued to look for her brother.

God, what am I going to do? If Catherine finds me, my life will be over and I will lose my son. Please help me find a way to stay hidden.

"I have a favor to ask of you."

"What is it, Countess?"

Margaret creased her eyebrows together in concern as she thought about what to do. She needed to find a way to make them go away. "I hate putting you in this position to help me with this problem. It could potentially place you in a dangerous situation."

"I put myself in danger daily by the line of work I choose to do. I would much rather put myself in danger for you."

She blushed, and he must have realized what his comment sounded like. "Excuse my boldness, my lady. I only meant that I am honored to help you."

She smiled and accepted his explanation. "I understand, and I thank you for your loyalty. I have an idea for a plan. What I need you to do is tell the people who are inquiring about me that I had been in France but left for Spain a month ago. It would explain away any information they found in France pointing to me being here, and hopefully, they will stop looking for me in France and move on to other places. Also, it would be good if you have a few other people give them the same information in a discreet manner."

"I will do it straightaway, my lady. I can also have my emissaries in Spain relay corresponding information when these men make their way there."

"Excellent, Monsieur Mulchere. I appreciate your help in this most precarious matter."

He grinned with admiration. "You are a smart one, my lady. Your plan should do a fine job of getting them off your track."

"That is the idea."

CHAPTER 8

*A*s Margaret put on a last dab of perfume, she contemplated her courtship by the Marquis de Badour. A few weeks had passed and her relationship with him was progressing, albeit slowly. Her confidence in their potential match was growing, as was her admiration for his character. The marquis had been taking her to church on a regular basis, and she could tell that his faith was an important part of his life by how he conducted himself as well as how he prayed over their meals and talked about God on their walks in the park.

Jackie entered the room with excitement radiating from her. "Good evening, chéri. Are you ready to be astounded? The French are said to do two things well, make love and make drama. How fortunate for you to be getting a bit of both."

Margaret knew that Jackie was referring to the fact that,

for the last couple of weeks, Pierre continued to make it clear that he planned to pursue her, despite the fact that she had been spending a great deal of time with the marquis. But Margaret did not want to think about any of that right now. Instead, she stood up and asked, "How do I look?"

She was feeling a bit self-conscious, wearing a dress that was off the shoulder and made of pure golden lace. The dress left very little to the imagination, but it went perfectly with the matching ivory, feathered mask the marquis had made for the masquerade ball to complement his own. She felt exposed in a way she had not encountered before, but she wanted to embrace the French style.

"Superb, Margaret, as always. The men will turn their heads when you enter the ballroom, as they always do. And I, I will just stand beside you, forgotten, following in your wake."

Jackie had a tendency to exaggerate. If the truth be known, Jackie had no problem attracting her own exuberant amount of attention. Margaret knew that she was only an English novelty and her appeal to the French nobility would soon wear off. The key was to land a good husband before that happened.

Margaret laughed. "I hardly think that you have anything to worry about. I hold no candle to you. Everyone knows that you are always the belle of the ball. What about the marquis's brother, Monte? He is most certainly interested in you."

"Well yes, although everyone says he was interested in

you first, but your mistreatment of him that first night at the opera made him turn to me."

"And who informed you of this fact?"

Jackie frowned. "Lady Ginene, and she hears everything."

Shrugging with a laugh, Margaret said, "Trust me, I have seen with my own eyes that he is interested in you and not me. Besides, he needs you to help mend his deflated pride after my rejection." She winked at her friend before continuing. "Come now, we both know that he only wanted to bed me. Lady Ginene only told you that to antagonize you. You know how she loves sticking her nose in other people's business and making up stories."

Jackie eyes narrowed in annoyance. "Oh, that wretched cow. I cannot believe that I actually listened to her pathetic lies. I am going to get her back, Margaret. I swear it."

Margaret smiled. "Good, there's my fiery friend. I am glad to see that you are back and ready for a fight."

"Yes, and I suppose that I do not mind so much, taking your castoffs, so long as they all look as good as Monte."

Grabbing her friend's hand, Margaret pulled her towards the door. "Jackie, my dear, you are never the receiver of secondhand men."

"You are right. It is my job to ruin them for *other* women. Besides, I heard a rumor that you will soon be spoken for, and when that happens, I will get my pick of the men again."

Margaret turned to face her friend and asked with excitement, "What have you heard?"

"Come now, we both know the marquis is completely

taken with you. Many hearts have been broken by the two of you taking up with each other."

"I will not apologize for that. I needed the right man to come along to want both me and my son. The marquis is a good man and will do right by both of us."

"I agree. He seems to make you happy?"

It was easy to hear the question at the end of her friend's statement. If she was honest with herself, she was comfortable with the marquis, but happy? She had come to the realization a long time ago that she would never truly be happy again after Henry's death. The most she could hope for was contentment. Margaret ignored the uneasiness she felt when thinking about her future with the marquis. Instead, she focused on the protection and safety he offered her family. It would have to be enough.

Less than an hour later, Margaret walked into the ballroom at the estate of Louis Audoux, the Comte de Delcambre. She was taken aback at the sheer grandness of the event. There were mountains of white marble and ornate gold decor as far as the eye could see, paired with beautiful tables with artfully arranged platters of lush fruits, quiches, and desserts. Servants with gleaming glass trays carrying crystal glasses filled with champagne were zigzagging through all the assembled guests who were decked out in stunning gowns and suits in variations of white, ivory, gold, and cream. It was the most lavish affair Margaret had ever attended. Giddy with anticipation of the upcoming festivities, she held her breath as she glanced around the room, looking for the marquis.

"He is not here yet."

Margaret froze in place. The last time someone had said that to her as she stood looking into a ballroom, it had ushered in the beginning of the end. Was that an omen? Was trouble on the horizon and she just could not see it yet? No, she did not believe in that sort of thing. It was just a coincidence.

She glanced up to see Pierre standing next to her.

"Is something wrong, Margaret?"

"No, I am entirely satisfactory."

He gently put his hand on the side of her arm and asked, "May I accompany you inside?"

Pulling away from his touch, she replied, "Jackie should be here any moment. I would not want to go in without her."

Frustrated by her withdrawal, he stated in a vexed tone, "What you mean is that you do not want the marquis to see us together again."

"It would make for an uncomfortable situation."

"For him, perhaps. It would please me, and I suspect it would you as well."

Agitated that he would not let her be, she replied tersely, "Pierre, you need to stop trying to force something between us that is never going to happen."

"I think you protest too much because you know it can and will.

"I think—"

But before she could respond, Jackie appeared, laughing and saying, "Look who I found in the entryway."

Walking beside her was Monte, and following in their wake was the marquis. He looked displeased to see Margaret and Pierre engaged in such an intimate conversation. He placed his hand under Margaret's elbow and said, "I was looking for you, Countess."

"You seem to have found her," Pierre said with a hint of sarcasm.

Ignoring Pierre, the marquis asked, "May I escort you inside, Lady Margaret?"

"But of course. I would be honored, Lord Robineau."

Margaret looked at the marquis with appreciation and avoided making eye contact with Pierre. As she walked with her arm looped through the marquis's, she noticed his attire for the evening and noted he looked debonair in his regal ivory suit. It had flecks of gold woven through, and he also donned a feathered mask in the same color. He specifically had his suit made to match her gown. As the couple made their way into the ballroom, many of the guests glanced their way. She knew that several of the women were extremely disappointed that the marquis had settled on her to court. She felt pressured to make sure he proposed before anything could stand in their way.

"Did I mention how dashing you look this eve, Lord Robineau?"

"Why thank you, Lady Margaret. I must say, you look exquisite in your gown."

The first song began to play as they took their places for the first dance. Margaret raised her gloved hand and gently rested it against the marquis's. As she looked into his eyes, she could see the esteem reflected back. She knew he respected her and cared for her, but was he capable of loving her?

He was unlike any of the other men she had fallen for in the past. All of them had professed their love quickly and openly. If the marquis felt anything for her beyond fondness, he kept it to himself. It unnerved her that she could not sense what he was feeling.

She hoped, by the end of the masquerade, she would amply convince him that he could not live without her. If that could happen, then maybe he could finally tell her he loved her.

Several dances passed and Margaret was trying to enjoy her evening with the marquis, but even though they got along sufficiently, there was a reserved nature between them that had not disappeared, despite all the time they had spent together. They had not even reached the phase in their relationship where they were using each other's given names. She wanted to bridge the distance between them but was unsure how to go about it. What was keeping them from progressing in their relationship?

God, help me to find a way to communicate better with the marquis. I want this relationship to work, but I need you to intervene. I do not know what I am doing wrong or why he seems so distant.

They continued to dance together for the rest of the waltz. When it ended, the marquis escorted Margaret over to where Jackie and Monte were sitting.

The conversation between the two of them was animated, and as Margaret and the marquis approached them, Jackie said, "Monte, you need to stop getting resentful every time another man asks me to dance. I thought we had agreed to keep this uncomplicated. You were the one who told me you did not want anything serious."

"That was in the beginning, but my feelings for you have changed. I want to pursue something more substantial with you."

"I find that flattering, but I am happy the way our arrangement is currently."

"Is it because I cannot offer you what other men can? Is it because I lack a title of my own as second-born son?"

"Monte, it has nothing to do with that. I have never let something like that influence my decisions."

"Then what? What is it that makes you capable of behaving this way?"

Jackie glanced to the side and looked at the young man uncomfortably standing nearby. "I am scheduled to dance with someone else for this song, and I need to take my leave."

"If you go to dance with him, Jackie, do not expect me to be waiting here for you if you return."

"What you choose to do is your choice, as what I choose to do is mine."

With that, Jackie stood up and extended her arm to the

gentleman next to her. He perfunctorily took her hand, avoiding making eye contact with Monte the entire time.

Margaret could see the seething anger in Monte's eyes. He looked as if he were going to explode at any moment. Monte turned his frustration on Margaret.

"What is wrong with your friend? How can she be so obtuse as to act the way she does?"

Margaret was shocked that he would be so bold as to say such offensive things about Jackie to her.

"I will not tolerate you talking to me about the vicomtesse that way."

"You will not 'tolerate' me talking about *her* that way? I could not care less what *you* will tolerate. It is I who should not tolerate you swooning all over my brother, who is clearly uninterested in you. If he truly were, it would be evidenced by a ring on your finger." Monte jerked her hand towards him and mockingly examined it. "No, I do not see one there. I find no evidence of him wanting to progress your relationship further."

Margaret yanked her hand away from Monte and forced herself not to respond. She glanced up to see the marquis's reaction, but she found no hint as to what he was thinking. If he cared for her, he should be interjecting, or at the least, as a gentleman, telling his brother to be respectful to her. Instead, he stood by silently and did nothing.

Mortified, she turned away and quickly left the ballroom. Was Monte right? Was she foolishly spending her energy on a man who was never going to commit to her? She felt so stupid for believing the marquis would ever want someone like her. Her past was too complicated, as was her future. He had said her having a child did not matter, but perhaps he had changed his mind. Perhaps he would rather be with a woman with no complications.

As she waited for her carriage to arrive to take her home, Margaret made herself hold back the tears threatening to fall. Why did she always pick the wrong men? She seemed to have a knack for it. If Mulchere was not still looking for her brother, she would be tempted to move forward with her plan and leave Europe permanently. But she could not leave, not until she was certain about what happened to her brother.

"Where will I be taking you, my lady?"

"She will not be needing your services tonight."

Margaret spun around to find Pierre standing behind her. "What are you doing here?"

"I came to make sure you are all right."

"Why? What did you hear?"

Pierre stepped forward and closed the space between them. He reached out and touched her cheek. "You look as if you are about to cry. Is this because of the marquis?"

"It does not matter. I was wrong about him."

"Why are you so willing to settle for a man who is not willing to fight for you?" He leaned in towards her and whispered, "I would fight for you, Margaret. I would fight until my dying breath."

"Pierre, you always say what I need to hear. I wish things could be different between us."

"They can be, Margaret. All you have to do is reach out and take what I am offering."

She looked up into his eyes. "What *are* you offering?"

"Me. All of me. Every inch of me, from my mind to my body."

"Pierre, I cannot go down this path with you. I value our friendship, but what we have cannot go beyond it."

"Why, Margaret? You keep rejecting my advances, but you never give me a reason."

"We are too different. I need to be with someone who believes in God as much as I do."

"You cannot be with me because I do not go to church?"

"That is not what I mean, and the fact that you think so makes my point for me. It is not about going to church. It is about what you believe, or rather, do not."

"I am sorry you feel that way, Margaret. We could be so brilliant together, but you keep running from it and making up excuses. You might want me to give up on the possibility of us, but I am not so easily dissuaded."

Margaret moved away from Pierre. "I am going for a walk. Do not follow me."

She rushed towards the estate's gardens and began to move through the maze of bushes. Her head was spinning with the mixture of how she felt about Pierre and the marquis. When she headed to the masquerade that night, she was positive the marquis was the right match for her. But

Pierre was right; he was not willing to fight for her. She had accepted that she might have to live without love, but she refused to live without a partner who would defend her.

God, please help me to see whether or not the marquis is the husband you want for me. I want to protect my family, but I also want to be content. I need you to guide me and show me what to do.

"Margaret, here you are."

She stopped moving when she heard the marquis's voice. She steadied herself and waited for him to continue with her back to him.

"I followed after you so that I could discuss what happened, but you were in conversation with the Vidame of Demoulin."

He gently pulled her around. "Why will you not face me?"

Tears hovered in the corner of her eyes. "Because I am exhausted. I am weary from fighting for something that is evidently more important to me than you."

"You think that? Was that what you and the vidame were talking about?" Was that jealousy she heard in his voice? If it was, it was the first time he ever demonstrated he was capable of being envious.

"What I talk to Pierre about is not any of your concern. As your brother pointed out, there is no commitment between us."

"My brother was wrong to talk to both you and the vicomtesse the way he did. He has a bad habit of attacking people when he does not get his way. I addressed the problem after you left, which is why I was delayed finding you."

"You defended me?"

"Categorically. You will be receiving an apology from my brother posthaste, as he has recognized the error he made tonight. Notwithstanding what you might believe, I want to continue courting you. I have always been cautious and move at a slower pace than most men do. I am sorry if that caused you to think I do not care. I do."

Margaret wanted to believe the marquis. She needed him to be telling the truth because she did not want to give up on their relationship, but it was hard for her to trust anyone after what happened to her back in England.

"I should have stopped him sooner, and I regret that. I have always had a hard time confronting my brother and keeping him in line. I am sorry that you were hurt by my lack of intervention. Can you forgive me?"

She looked at the marquis for several seconds before saying, "You did hurt me. I can forgive you this time, but do not do something like that again. I will not be with someone who will not fight for me."

"I am not a fighter by nature, but for you, I will make it my ambition to become one."

CHAPTER 9

*H*enry was lying on a blanket on the garden grass as Margaret gently tickled him and listened to his giggles. He was smiling now and pointing to everything. She loved how everything fascinated him as he was seeing it all for the first time.

She heard approaching footsteps and looked up to see Francisca headed in her direction. She had an apprehensive look on her face and her hands were folded in front of her as she came to a stop in front of Margaret.

"My lady, I was hoping to have a chance to talk with you about something."

"Certainly, Francisca. You know you are welcome to discuss anything with me."

"Thank you, my lady. I know you are aware a local merchant has been wooing me the past couple of months."

"Of course. You asked my permission for the time off to spend with him."

"Our relationship has developed, and he wants to ask for my hand in marriage. I do not have a father to ask, and he wanted to know if he could ask you, as you are the closest thing I have to family."

Margaret stood up and asked, "Is he here now?"

"Yes. He is outside presently."

"I am flattered you feel that away about me. I would be honored to give my blessing."

Francisca nodded, spun around, and headed back the way she came. A few minutes later, she returned with a young man of average build and looks. He appeared nervous, and Margaret smiled at him to try to relieve some of the tension.

He bowed awkwardly, and as he came up, he said, "Good afternoon, Countess. My name is Hugo Millet. Francisca has told me that she informed you of my intentions. I have come to care deeply for her, and since she came to France from England with you, I wanted to ask your permission to marry her."

"Hugo—I hope you do not mind me calling you that—you do not need my consent, but I would be pleased to give you my blessing. I have never seen Francisca happier than I have in the past few months since she has developed a relationship with you. I wish you both all the joy in the world."

"Thank you, Lady Margaret. I appreciate all you have done for me, and I am so glad that, through my service to you, I was able to meet Hugo and fall in love."

Francisca hugged Hugo, and as he wrapped his arms around her shoulders and kissed her forehead, Margaret could see the love between them.

~

Margaret was exhausted from a long night with Jackie and the Robineau brothers, after Monte had apologized to both Margaret and Jackie. Both women chose to forgive him, which led to the reconciliation between Jackie and Monte.

She had thoroughly enjoyed herself with the marquis, but she found herself constantly thinking about Pierre throughout the night. She watched him from across the room to see who he was talking to and with whom he shared his next dance. Every time another woman flirted with him or made him laugh, Margaret could feel the jealousy she knew she should not feel surface.

Her attention should have been on the marquis, as he was the man she hoped to marry soon. She knew she cared for him, but the attraction she wanted to feel for him lay dormant while she was persistently fighting her attraction for Pierre.

Margaret checked in on her son in his nursery before heading towards her chambers. Margaret made her way over to his crib and marveled at how serene he looked, lying there fast asleep. She reached out to touch his brown curly locks of hair that fell across his forehead. He was the best thing in her life and she loved him dearly. She leaned forward and kissed him softly on his cheek. After a few more moments of watching him slumber, she nodded at Sarah to take over watching him as she quietly left the room.

After heading down the corridor to her rooms, Margaret sat down at her vanity to allow Motty to prepare her for bed. As the girl went about removing the pins from her hair and combing it out, Margaret reflected on the night's activities.

Margaret stood up to allow her servant to remove her dress and corset and replace it with her nightgown and robe.

"Thank you, Motty. That will be all I require for the night."

As the girl left Margaret's chambers, she took out a book to read by the fireplace in her sitting room. She had gotten hooked on the popular French novellas that were the new fashion to read. They were silly stories about love and how to succeed in the game of it. She found the idea of them to be ostentatious, but somehow, she could not stop reading them.

Captivated by a passage about using love as an art form and how to "paint" the perfect picture, Margaret slightly jumped when a soft knock came at the door.

She stood up and put the book on her chair, then walked over to the door. Thinking it was Sarah, she opened it but was shocked to find Pierre standing on the other side instead. It was quite late for him to be visiting, and even more surprising since his suite was on the other side of the estate.

He looked at her for a moment, then asked, "May I come in?"

She did not answer right away, but after a few seconds stepped aside so he could enter.

Pierre looked around and smiled. "I do not think I have even been in these rooms."

She laughed. "You have not even seen all of your own estate?"

He shook his head and said half-seriously, "I have too many of them to spend the time."

She gestured for him to sit down across from her. She picked the book up off her chair and placed it on the table between them.

Glancing at it, Pierre commented, "I see my cousin has enticed you into reading one of those new books about love. Tell me, do you find it as intriguing as she does?"

Margaret nodded. "I have to admit, despite my best efforts, I find them riveting. From my own experiences, love is not all it is made out to be, so I find it amusing to read about people so caught up in finding it."

"What do you mean?"

"I mean, first it lures you in and then, once you are trapped in its grasp, it rips you apart. Nothing good comes of it."

"Not all love is like that."

Smiling with motherly love, Margaret agreed. "True, my love for my son is pure and is not like that. But love between a man and a woman exacts too high a price for my liking."

"I could change your mind about it," he said, smiling sensually.

"Perhaps you could, but we will never know as I have no intentions of ever experiencing any of it ever again."

Pierre arched his eyebrows, saying, "I would think that after being married and having your 'experiences' cut so unexpectedly short that you would indeed want to have more of them." He looked at her with a deeper meaning and said, "And new ones."

Standing up like a lynx uncurling, he walked over to her, reached down, and yanked her up into his arms. As he leaned forward, he pressed his lips firmly against her own.

She was surprised Pierre was able to get past her defenses. When she did not resist, he deepened the kiss. Margaret wrapped her arms around his neck and leaned into him. It felt good to be held again.

Pierre ran his hands down Margaret's back and started to kiss her in other places, making trails down her neck and across her face. He pulled her in tighter with the other arm that was wrapped around her waist.

Even though she knew she wanted to be close to him, Margaret stopped Pierre before it became too late by gently pulling away and saying, "I think it is time for us to say good night, Pierre."

She watched as he fought to bring his desire under control. Then he stepped back and nodded in acceptance. He stared at her intensely for several moments before he took her hand and kissed the top of it.

Slowly, he raised his eyes to meet hers, then asked softly,

"Are you sure what you want is for me to say good night, Margaret?"

Pierre was still holding her hand, and for some reason, she did not find herself pulling away as quickly as she knew she should be.

He started to move in towards her again, but before his body came to rest next to hers, Margaret quickly raised a hand and placed it on his chest as she shook her head.

But Pierre chose to ignore her weak protest and rested his own hand over the top of hers on his chest. He moved into her and placed his other hand under her chin, whispering, "Let me stay, Margaret. I know we both want me to."

She looked up to meet Pierre's eyes and tried to muster the words to send him away. But somehow she was finding herself drowning in the dark, bottomless pools of splendor they held instead.

"You are so beautiful, Margaret. I do not think I have ever wanted anything more than to be with you right now."

He tipped his head down quickly before she could react and claimed her lips with his own again. This kiss was more fervent than the previous one. There was almost a desperation in it that felt as if, at any moment, he knew she could stop him.

Pierre pulled her in close to him and Margaret gasped against his lips, which caused Pierre to moan with intensity in response.

Warning bells went off in Margaret's head. She had allowed him to kiss her again because it had been sudden, not letting her think about her response. Added with the fact that it had been so long since she had felt a man's touch, she realized that it was true—she did crave it.

But from the quaking she was feeling inside, she knew she was headed into dangerous territory. That time, Margaret placed both hands on Pierre's chest and firmly pushed away. Quickly, she averted her eyes, knowing that she would only see disappointment reflected back from Pierre.

Margaret swallowed the lump that had formed in her throat and said firmly, "Good night, Pierre."

Without a word, he turned around to leave.

With his back to her and his hand on the doorknob, Pierre whispered, "I wish you would not push me away."

And with that, he walked out the door.

CHAPTER 10

*T*he next morning, Margaret told Jackie of her plans to get a place of her own. She knew her new arrangements would be inferior to her current living conditions, considering her limited resources, but she had imposed on Pierre for far longer than she intended.

"I do not see why you have to move out of Pierre's estate. He is a perfect gentleman and he will remain so."

"Yes, Jackie, but I need to do this. It is time for Henry and I to get a place of our own. Pierre has been wonderful these last few months, but things are getting too complicated between us. Besides," she said as she put the last of her dresses in the trunk, "my temporary stay here in France is turning out to be a permanent one."

"Well, then, you should move in with me." Jackie put her arm around Margaret's shoulder and said, "You are like my sister, and I hate the thought of you staying alone."

"I hardly think so. I do not want to cramp your style. I know how you love to 'entertain' gentlemen. We would just be in the way. Anyhow, we will not be alone because we have Sarah, Albert, and Motty."

"They are servants. It is different. You need someone of your own kind."

Margaret chose not to argue the point that Sarah was her oldest friend and had supported her through countless difficult times. Instead, she only said, "I will be sufficient on my own, I promise."

"Still, I do not think you need to move out." She paused a moment, then continued, "Have you told Pierre yet?"

Shaking her head as she finished packing, Margaret replied, "No, I did not know how to tell him, and I know he is going to fight me on it."

"You see, it is that simple. You should stay."

Turning around, Margaret sighed. "I am moving out and that is final. I will not be far away, and you can come calling any time. You know that."

"I do and I will."

"Now I suppose it is time for me to go tell Pierre of my plans. Wish me luck."

Giving Margaret a supportive hug, Jackie asserted, "Good luck. You are going to need it to convince Pierre."

As Margaret made her way through Pierre's estate to tell him of her plans to move out, she thought about what occurred between them the night before. If she had let herself, she could have easily let Pierre stay with her as he asked. The fact that he could effortlessly tempt her to do something so reckless reminded her of her past with the duke. Softly, Margaret rapped on the door to Pierre's study.

"You may enter."

Pierre looked up from the stack of papers in front of him on his desk as Margaret entered the room. The sullen look on his face was immediately replaced by a look of cheerfulness.

"Why, this is a welcome surprise. To what do I owe the honor of your presence this morning, Margaret?"

She tightened her lips in worry before saying, "I have something to talk to you about that I feel cannot wait for a later time."

With a hopeful tone, Pierre asked, "Have you changed your mind about us?"

"On the contrary. Due to what has transpired between us, I find it sagacious that I remove myself from your estate immediately."

Standing up, Pierre came around to the front of his desk. The strain on his face was palpable. It was obvious he was trying to keep his emotions under control.

"If this is because of last night, Margaret, I give you my word that it will never happen again unless you want it."

"I admit, last night did frighten me, but there are many more reasons why I must move out beyond what happened."

He took her chin in his hand and pulled her face up, making her eyes meet his own. "Give me one legitimate reason as to why you should leave, Margaret."

"Pierre, we both know it is indecent for me to be here in the first place. I am a widow, and I should not be staying with an unwed man. When I was staying here in secret, it was one thing because no one was aware, but now that I have started to circulate in French society, it is not seemly. Even though nothing is going on between us, no one else knows that."

Looking at her meaningfully, he asked, "Is there nothing going on between us?"

Pulling free from his grasp, Margaret replied, "Of course, there is nothing going on."

"Then why did you kiss me back last night?"

She tapped her foot in annoyance at having to exam the whole situation again.

"Because, unfortunately, my stupid desires have always run rampant and caused havoc in my life. They seem to have a mind of their own."

Margaret glanced at him and saw his utter look of devotion for her on his face. No matter what she did, he was not going to back down. Unless… she hated that it came to this, but she realized now that the only way she was going to make him let her go was if she drove him out of her life.

"You must not take it to heart. It is nothing that *you* did. I just react that way when *any* man touches me."

He frowned. "I do not believe you. I know there is a difference when I am with you. I merely touch you and I feel you lean into it. Do you also do that with all men?"

She shrugged, trying to avoid admitting the truth. "I do

not notice it. And yes, I do probably do that with all men. I am very fickle when it comes to my emotions." Part of her believed what she was saying about herself; if he knew about her whole past with the duke and Henry, Pierre would realize that she was unable to stay devoted to one man for any real length of time. If he knew the truth about her past in all the gory details, that would be the end of it. Preparing herself to ruin his idealistic images of her, she said softly, "If you really knew me and what I've done in my past, Pierre, you would realize why we cannot be together."

"What? What have you done that is so terrible that I will no longer want you?"

"I told you about my past and how the Duke of Witherton forced himself on me. What I did not tell you is that before I was married to Henry, I had thought myself in love with the duke. He pursued me, and I let him even though I was betrothed to Henry. Even on my wedding day, mere moments before I married my intended, I let him kiss me outside the chapel."

He stood up and reached out quickly, taking her into his arms before she knew what was happening. "It is not going to work, you trying to persuade me that you are a bad person. I know you, Margaret, and you are one of the kindest and most trustworthy people I know. You will not get rid of me that easily."

Pierre dipped his head down and allowed his mouth to hover just inches from Margaret as he whispered against her skin, "Tell me you do not want me to kiss you, and I will stop."

She knew she should object since she was being courted by the marquis, but she could not offer up the words. Somehow Pierre made it impossible for her to think clearly once he touched her.

When she did not protest, he seized her lips with his own, declaring that she was his for the taking. It was demanding but kind and tender all at the same time. Her mind said to pull away quickly, but her heart and body betrayed her and wanted to let him kiss her a little longer.

She whimpered as he deepened the kiss and clung to the front of his shirt. His kisses were the most mesmerizing thing she had ever felt. He was right; when he touched her, it was like a wildfire being lit.

Margaret was slowly losing control of her own desires again, and she could not let that happen. She pushed against his chest and broke free of his embrace. Stepping back, she said, "That is the reason that I must leave. For I fear, if I stay here, you would be my undoing."

He licked his lips and replied, "Perhaps you are right, but right now, all I can think about is kissing you again."

And with that, he grabbed her and took possession of her mouth once more. But that time, Margaret steadied herself, and with every ounce of self-control, she did not allow herself to return his kiss. Instead, she stood completely still and did nothing.

After a few moments of no response, reluctantly, he let her go.

As he looked at her with eyes smoldering with desire, she said, "And that is why I must leave."

Margaret turned and fled the room.

CHAPTER 11

*A*fter enjoying a delicious dinner at one of the local restaurants, Margaret was drinking a dessert port while sitting next to the marquis. They were accompanied by Monte and Jackie, who had gotten into a fight the previous night but made up later the same evening. Honestly, it was hard for Margaret to keep track of when they were seeing each other and when they were not. Their "relationship" was constantly shifting.

At the current moment, Margaret watched the other couple nestled in a corner of the room, engaged in an intimate lovers' conversation. For all the potential volatility in their relationship, Margaret still envied the passion. From her experience, it did not seem possible to have both stability and passion coexist without it erupting. Jackie was the complete opposite of Margaret when it came to what she wanted in a relationship. She would forgo stability for passion, while Margaret needed stability above all else for her son's sake.

Margaret turned her attention back to the marquis and broke the silence. "My lord, we have been spending considerable time together. I think it is about time that you meet my son. Would you care to go for a walk with us in the park?"

The marquis stared at Margaret for several seconds, revealing nothing on his face, before saying, "I find that suggestion... agreeable."

The pause in his response did not lend Margaret to believe he was enthusiastic about her invitation. Did he not want to meet her son and get to know him? If he were to wed Margaret, he would become Henry's father by marriage. She hoped he would want to take an active role in the boy's life. Did he view it as just another step towards reaching his goal of winning her hand? She did not want him to view marrying her as return on an investment but as the prize for making the effort in getting to know her.

"If you feel it too soon, we can delay it, or postpone such an interaction altogether."

He furrowed his brows together in confusion. "I thought I was clear. I am not opposed to meeting your son."

Margaret tried to disguise her frustration, but she found it hard to communicate with the marquis at times. One moment, he was engrossed in her, and the next, he seemed distant. He was disconnected from her in a way she could not explain. Was she forcing something that was not there?

"Would tomorrow afternoon be agreeable? Say around two o'clock?"

"I will be there."

She watched the marquis as the next course of the meal was placed before them. He seemed especially distracted, as if something was keeping him for concentrating on their time together.

It was unlike Margaret to be so forward, but she needed to understand what was going on with him and why he detached from her. "My lord, is something amiss? You seem preoccupied this eve."

The marquis focused his attention on her and, as if seeing her for the first time all evening, reached out and patted the side of her arm. "I am sorry. There has been a situation that I have been dealing with for a considerable amount of time, and today it escalated."

How vague. She asked him a direct question and he gave her an answer that only created more questions. What situation, and who did it involve? She wondered if he had a mistress. It was not uncommon for noblemen to have one, and she would not be surprised if that were the case. She did not like it, but they were not engaged. Presently, she did not have a right to be upset about it.

"I am sorry to hear that, Lord Robineau. Perhaps I can help if you discuss the details with me."

He adamantly shook his head. "As I said, I have been

dealing with this particular situation for a substantial time. Discussing it will not change anything."

Secrets. Just like the duke, just like Henry. Why did every man she became involved with keep secrets from her? As Margaret was about to object, a server entered the room and came over to them. He handed the marquis a folded piece of paper, which he in turn opened and hastily read.

The marquis quickly glanced up at Margaret and stated with trepidation in his voice, "I have an urgent matter to which I must attend. I am sorry for my brash departure, but it cannot wait."

The marquis rose to his feet, nodded towards Margaret, and exited the room.

Shocked by the marquis's uncharacteristic frazzled behavior, Margaret sat still and considered what just occurred. What was going on that would cause him to act in such a way?

Monte came over to where Margaret sat and looked at the empty seat next to her. "Where did my brother go?"

"He did not say. He received a note and left abruptly. You would not happen to know what matter caused such alarm, would you?"

Monte turned ghostly pale and said, "I need to be going as well."

Margaret watched as the younger brother rushed out after the other. What would cause both men to act that way? The marquis was altruistic, but she had never seen Monte care about anything that did not give him pleasure.

It seemed peculiar that both men would act in such a manner.

Jackie approached Margaret and asked, "What in the devil got into those Robineau brothers?" It seemed something tied both men together that neither she nor Jackie was aware of.

"I do not know, but I intend to find out."

The park was picturesque with the green grass and trees and the flowers in bloom. Many Parisians were out, strolling along the walking paths that weaved through the park's natural splendor. Margaret remembered reading about the construction of the new parks and boulevards when Napoleon III became emperor. Jean-Charles Adolphe Alphand had designed the parks to accommodate both horseback riders and walkers along the paths, making promenading one of the new favorite pastimes for city dwellers.

Looking down at Henry in his baby carriage, Margaret gently adjusted the blanket around his body. He had been fast asleep for the past hour, as the motion from the constant rolling lulled him to slumber.

She had reached the place where the marquis was supposed to meet her. It was fifteen past two, and he was never late. What was keeping him?

Margaret fluffed out and arranged the crinoline of her soft blue velvet dress as she sat on one of the park benches that adorned the walking paths. She watched as the many families, couples, and groups of friends strolled past her. They all seemed so happy, decked out in their finest outfits and enjoying one another's company. At times, she felt she was just like them, but underneath her content exterior, something always seemed like it was missing.

"Good afternoon, Lady Margaret."

She looked up to see the marquis standing next to her. "Would you care to take a walk with me?"

"Yes, my lord." She extended her hand to the marquis, who took it and helped her to her feet. Margaret waved Sarah over and handed the baby carriage to her.

"Henry is asleep. When he wakes up, please bring him back to us so that I may introduce him to Lord Robineau."

"Of course, my lady."

The marquis took Lady Margaret's hand and placed it in the crook of his arm, saying, "I wanted to apologize again for what occurred last night, Lady Margaret. I did not want to leave you in the fashion I did."

"Did everything resolve with the situation?"

He nodded. "Temporarily."

"You mean it will happen again?"

"Unfortunately."

She felt as if they were talking around a subject she did not have enough knowledge about to understand. It was uncomfortable, and she did not like it.

"My lord, do you trust me?"

He looked over at her and smiled. "Assuredly."

"Then why will you not tell me what is going on with your situation?" She did not expect to be so direct with the marquis, but she was tired of allowing him to be evasive.

"It is more complex than you can imagine."

"I want you to know you can confide in me without apprehension. I am an excellent secret keeper."

"I appreciate your sincerity, and I do believe you. However, the situation does not involve me alone."

His circumstance involved someone else. She had previously wondered if he had a mistress. He did not seem the type, but one could never know. She hoped it was not the case, because depending on the depth of the relationship, it could pose a potential problem for her down the road. She did not want to enter a marriage where she was competing with another woman for the rest of her life. There was also the possibility that he had an illegitimate child. It was more common than revealed in their social circles. Did he think she could not love another woman's child? She hoped he knew she would care for anyone who was important to the marquis.

They walked in silence until Sarah approached them with the baby carriage. "My lady, Henry is awake now. Would you like me to get him out for you?"

Margaret shook her head. "No, I can manage myself, Sarah. Please, wait for us over by the bench."

"Of course, my lady."

Henry smiled as Margaret's face came into view. She

lifted the small boy out of the carriage and turned him to face the marquis.

"May I introduce to you Lord Henry Wellesley."

Breaking the formality of the moment, Henry giggled and swatted at the marquis's nose. The marquis's eyes grew wide with surprise, and as he looked from the baby to Margaret, a giant grin crossed his face. They all began to laugh.

Margaret turned Henry back towards her and said, "You adorable boy. Do you know how much I love you? More than all the stars in the sky." She tried to place Henry back in the baby carriage, but he would have none of it. His little head popped up over the edge with both his hands on either side of his face. He peered out over the side and he wrinkled his nose up in a tiny tooth-exposing grin. He dropped his head down again, and a few moments later, his little head popped up once more.

"Are you wanting to play peek-a-boo, Henry?"

Bending down, Margaret covered her eyes with her hands, waited several seconds, then cracked one side, and Henry faintly laughed. She cracked the other side and he giggled harder. She swiftly pulled both hands away and his whole little body shook with amusement.

"Do you think you two are the only ones who know how to play this game? I used to play it all the time with my brother and sister," the marquis confessed.

He bent down and went through the same pattern with the baby. Henry was skeptical of the stranger at first, but after the second attempt, the marquis received the same results as Margaret.

"You are wonderful with him, my lord. It does my heart good to see you interact so well with him. You mentioned playing games with your siblings. I knew you had a brother, but I was unaware you had a sister."

"Yes, though unfortunately, she is no longer with us."

"Oh, I am so sorry. I did not mean to pry."

"You did not. It was I who mentioned her. It is hard for me sometimes to accept that she is gone. The three of us were tremendously close before she left us. You see, I was the oldest and took care of my younger siblings after our parents died."

It explained so much about the marquis's personality and why he always seemed to be taking care of Monte. Monte was the only family the marquis had left, and he must feel responsible for him. The loss of a parent was difficult, but the loss of a sibling was unique beyond comparison.

A gloomy look took over Margaret's face. "I understand your loss, probably more than most. I, too, lost a sibling, a twin brother, when we were ten. Not a day goes by that I do not miss him immensely."

"I am sorry to hear about your brother, Lady Margaret. It seems you have had a great deal of loss for someone so young."

"I have, but I choose not to dwell on it. I would rather focus on the future."

He waited several moments before asking, "Would you care to join me for dinner tomorrow evening at my home?"

"It would be my pleasure to have dinner with you."

"I will send my carriage to pick you up tomorrow night at seven o'clock."

Margaret was hopeful that the marquis planned to propose to her the following night. Inviting her to his home was an intimate act and the sign she had been waiting for that a proposal was forthcoming.

CHAPTER 12

The carriage pulled up to the marquis's home, which was grand beyond all measure. A stack of four marble pillars stood on each side of the massive French doors that were made out of pure mahogany. The garden areas surrounding the home were precisely manicured and rich in tropical vegetation. It was rumored that he was the wealthiest of all the noblemen in Paris. At times, she thought people were exaggerating for her benefit, but as she marveled at the vastness of his estate, she realized that he was substantially more wealthy than she had even imagined.

Margaret gave her hand to the footman who helped her out of the carriage. As she stood, she tried to smooth out the wrinkles in her dress. She was wearing a sea-green gown that was translucent and hinted at bare flesh underneath. The bodice was accented with rows of iridescent pearls and had matching cap sleeves which draped elegantly over her shoulders. It was one of Worth's creations, the most notable dressmaker in all of Europe, and she had saved it the whole time she had been in France for a special occasion. She hoped tonight would be the night the marquis was going to finally ask her to be his wife.

She ascended the steps to the marquis's home and breathed deeply before she knocked. Margaret prayed. *God, please make clear to me whether or not I am supposed to be with Michel. I want to be in your will and do what is right. Help me make the right decision.*

Within moments, the doors opened and a short, stout butler with thinning grey hair stood on the other side.

"Please enter, Countess. The marquis will be down shortly."

The entryway was every bit as stately as she expected. There was an enormous crystal chandelier hanging from the center, and several pieces of stunning antique furnishings were placed considerately around the room. Breathtaking paintings hung on the walls, which accented the furniture flawlessly. Margaret could tell from being in the room that it had been decorated by a woman. She wondered who.

"Good evening, Lady Margaret," the marquis said as he came down the stairs to greet her.

"Good evening, my lord. Thank you for your invitation."

"I am glad that you are here. I have wanted to show you my home for some time now."

If that were true, why had he waited so long to invite her? She understood protocol and why waiting a respectable amount of time to make their relationship official was important, but he had been moving at a glacial pace. This whole time, she thought he had invited her to dinner to propose, but perhaps it was just the opposite. Had he found out about her past and decided to deal with her in private to avoid a scene?

She needed to take her mind off all the swirling questions in her mind. "My lord, the furnishings in your home are exquisite. I cannot imagine you having the time to acquire all of them. Who managed to procure such lovely pieces?"

The marquis took her by the hand and led her past the dining room towards the back hall of his home.

"I have something to share with you. It is of a private nature, and only my trusted staff and brother are aware of the situation."

Where could he be taking her? This was not at all what she expected to happen tonight. She thought they would have a lovely dinner, delightful conversation, and then he would ask her to marry him. Instead, he was leading her down a dark hallway to show her something that sounded as if it would irrevocably change the dynamic of their relationship.

What could it be? Did he have some peculiar tendencies? Was he wanting to share with her his unusual bedroom requisites before making a commitment to her? If that was the case, she needed to stop him now before this went any further.

"My lord, if you plan to show me your private necessities,

I am sorry to say, I cannot accommodate you."

He stopped for a moment and looked at her, furrowing his brows together in bafflement. As he realized what she was suggesting, he shook his head in denial and said, "I think you misunderstand what I am trying to tell you. It is my fault, as I am not being clear. I thought I would be calm when doing this, but instead, I feel anxious. This could change everything between us."

They stood outside a door, and nervously, the marquis opened it. Inside, the room was barely lit by a few candles and a fire inside the hearth. As they stepped into the room, Margaret noticed a young woman lying in bed. She appeared to be asleep.

"This is my sister, Marie. She has been here with me since her accident three years ago. To protect the family's name, we informed everyone that she had passed away. It was simpler than explaining the truth."

Margaret stared at the women who looked no older than her. She was beautiful with long brown hair and olive-colored skin. Something was not right though, because even though the marquis had been talking, the young woman did not stir.

"What happened to her?"

"She was riding one of our horses and was thrown from it. She hit her head on a tree and lost consciousness. The doctors tried everything they could but little function returned. They say it is permanent and she will live the rest of her life in this state."

"I am so sorry, my lord. This must be so difficult."

"I have adjusted to the situation. The servants take excellent care of her, but if we are to move forward, I felt you needed to know."

This explained so much of the marquis's behavior. Why he seemed preoccupied so often, why he had never invited her to his home before, why he never spoke of family. Then she realized it also explained why he had left the other night the way he did.

"*This* is the situation you had to attend to the other night?"

"Yes, Marie had a convulsion spell and the doctor thought we might lose her. She had them earlier in the day, but he had thought he had calmed her. I would not have left her had I thought otherwise."

Margaret gently touched the marquis's cheek with her gloved hand. "Of course, you would not have left her. You always think of others first."

He shrugged. "It is in my nature to take care of others. I have a deep desire to protect the ones I love."

The more she got to know the marquis, the more she admired him. He was a such a kind and sincere man, and his loyalty was without measure.

"I am perplexed by something you said. Why did your family's name need protection? Why did you pretend she was dead?"

"She was not alone when the incident happened. She had run away to be with one of the stable boys because she was with child. She lost the baby through the accident. The scandal would have ruined my family."

"You made the best choice you could under the circumstances. Thank you for trusting me enough to share this with me."

"I will understand if this makes you think differently about allowing me to court you. She comes as part of the compendium with choosing to be with me. It is a significant burden to ask anyone else to accept. It is one of the reasons I wanted to assess your character fully before even broaching the subject. But when I saw you engage with your son yesterday, I knew you were capable of deep compassion."

"In regards to how I feel after finding this out, I do not want to end our courtship. It is just the opposite. I hope it will continue to completion. Your dedication to your sister only proves to me that you are a committed and faithful gentleman. It renews my trust in you."

"I am glad you feel as such. Dinner will be ready, and I suspect you are famished, as am I. I think we should make our way back to my dining hall."

"Of course, my lord."

"I think, after all that has been revealed this evening, it is time that you start addressing me as Michel."

"Thank you, and please call me Margaret."

"I can honestly say you know all of my secrets now. We can move forward with nothing between us."

Margaret wanted to tell the marquis about her past, but the idea of telling him and having him no longer care for her made her blood run cold. She had grown to care for him, and she did not want him to look at her as if she were tainted. She felt it about herself, and if she did, she had no doubt he would feel the same.

"I wish to move forward with our courtship as well."

A strange expression of uncertainty seemed to float across Michel's face, but as quickly as it appeared, it was gone. Margaret wondered what he was thinking to cause such a manifestation. Did he know about the details of her past? He had told her once that he had asked about her past and knew she was widowed, but had he found out the particulars surrounding how it happened?

"Is something bothering you?"

"Is there anything you would like to share with me, Margaret?"

"You know everything there is to know about me that is of merit."

"I hope you know you can trust me as well, Margaret. I want you to feel safe with me."

"I do feel safe with you, Michel. From the first moment I met you and you rescued me from the mugger, I knew you would keep me from harm."

"I am glad to hear it. I find myself having the deepest desire to keep you protected at all costs."

"Thank you, Michel. It means the world to me." She wanted to tell him the whole story about her past, but she could not take the chance that he would end their relationship over it. She needed him more than the risk was worth.

CHAPTER 13

 argaret had been in France just shy of a
year, and she was now part of the most elite
circles, being invited to all the grandest social functions. She
barely had time to breathe.

That evening, Michel had gotten them invitations to the
prestigious ball at Tuileries Palace in honor of Spanish Queen
Isabella II's visit to France. The host and hostess were Emperor
Napoleon III and Empress Eugenie, and only the most select
nobility and members of French society were going to be
guests. Margaret had never attended a ball at a palace before or
attended a function with royalty and heads of state. Secretly,
she was nervous she might make a mistake when being introduced and embarrass herself, or worse, Michel.

After picking up her gloves, beaded clutch, and shawl,
Margaret headed towards the front of her new residence.

Pierre had made sure that when she moved out she had one of the finest estates in the city. He paid a full year for the upkeep and staff. She had protested, but he explained that it was already done. Realizing her finances were dismal to say the least, she grudgingly accepted his offer. If she was careful, the money she had brought with her from England would last her until she married the marquis.

She took one last look at her fitted corset and crinoline dress in the entry hallway mirror, making sure that all the gold tassels and fringe layers along the bottom layers of the dark burgundy dress were in place. She adjusted her gold and opal jewelry that adorned her ears, throat, and wrist, gifts from the marquis.

"You look exceptional tonight."

Margaret saw Michel's reflection in the mirror and smiled.

"Thank you, Michel. I did not hear you come inside."

"I wanted to watch you come down the stairs. It seems I was too late."

Ever since the night he opened up to her about his sister, she had seen a tenderness and romantic side emerge from the marquis. Michel was surprising her more and more, and she realized that he was a brilliant counterpart. He provided security and companionship for her, and he would be a good father to Henry.

She still missed her late husband every day and wished he could have known his son and raised him, but life did not work out that way. Michel would do right by both of them, and she needed to live for the future, not in the past.

The only thing that could spoil the evening was if Pierre decided to make an appearance at her side. Even though she did not encourage it, he continued to make it clear that he was still interested in her.

It had been hard seeing Pierre after leaving his home the way she had. Every time, he seemed to be doing worse with her rejection. It hurt her that she had caused him pain, but it was far better for her to do it now than down the road.

She hated hurting Pierre, but she had decided what would be best for her as well as her son. The marquis could protect Henry, and right now, that seemed to be the most pressing issue. In the back of her mind, she was always secretly worried that either Catherine or Witherton would find her and everything she had built for herself in France would be destroyed. The only way to protect her family was to marry someone who could keep them safe and not allow anyone to get close enough to harm them.

"Monte and Jackie are waiting for us in the carriage." Michel reached out his hand to her and Margaret placed hers in it.

"Are you as ecstatic as Jackie to attend the emperor's ball? She has talked about nothing else since we picked her up."

Margaret tightened her lips together in worry. "To be truthful, I am more nervous than excited."

"You, nervous? Whatever for?"

"What if I make a fool of myself? What if I make a fool of you?"

"Margaret, do not be ridiculous. You are anything but a fool."

"But I could trip while I curtsey or stumble my words when I speak to the emperor and empress."

"You were born to be amongst these people. I have never seen anyone take so well to French society."

He always had such a way of making her feel secure. His calming nature was her favorite attribute.

As they climbed into the carriage, Jackie said, "Margaret, can you believe in just a few moments you will be meeting the emperor and empress? I mean, I have met them before on several occasions, but this is your *first* time meeting the imperial family."

What had started out as nervousness in the pit of her stomach was now turning into downright queasiness. She had not felt like this since her first ball on her sixteenth birthday.

"Are you all right, Margaret?"

She nodded with her eyes closed. Keeping them open made it worse, especially when she felt every bump as they rode along the cobblestone road to the palace.

"Do we need to pull over so you can get out and rest a moment?"

"No, I am satisfactory. I am trying to remain composed."

Margaret laid her head on Michel's shoulder and rode the

rest of the way with her eyes shut. She absentmindedly heard the conversation going on around her.

Trying to ignore them, Margaret prayed quietly to herself. *Lord, give me peace right now and be with me this evening. I really do not want to make an idiot of myself or humiliate Michel. Help me to make a good first impression and keep anything bad from happening this evening.*

She opened her eyes just as their carriage came to a stop in front of the palace. She heard Jackie exclaim, "Breathtaking! I never get used to coming here, not even after all these years of attending the emperor's balls."

The prominent building had a massive squared dome in the center with ornate curved architectural features. Light illuminated from the many windows that lined the front of the impressive citadel. The palace's footmen opened the carriage doors and helped the women out, the men following behind. Margaret looked around at the other carriages filled with nobles, famous actors and actresses, artists, and bankers. All the guests displayed their most ostentatious attire and were drenched in their finest jewels, wanting to make the grandest impression on the imperial family.

As they ascended the stairs, Margaret made herself slowly take in deep breaths to steady her nerves. She did not want to pass out. She had heard that it did happen on occasion, and she did not want to be known as one of *those* women.

They entered the lavishly decorated Grande Galerie of the palace, and Margaret drew in a deep breath, holding it. It was magnificent. She could not believe her eyes with all the gold inlayed furnishings with opulent upholstery and exquisite details. Elaborate tapestries hung on the walls and windows, and the crystal chandeliers glistened, as did the marble floors.

"Are you ready for this, Margaret?" Michel asked.

"As I will ever be."

As they moved forward in the processional line, she heard different names and titles called out. The closer they reached, the more details she could make out. The empress was of petite size and was quite striking in looks with an oval face, kind brown eyes, and heart-shaped lips. Her dark brown hair was pulled back and parted down the center with a delicate gold and sapphire crown on top. She wore a soft blue crinoline dress with a gold sash that lay across her chest. The emperor seemed more reserved than the empress and had a firm look on his face. His dark brown hair was parted on the right side and curled slightly on the edges near his ears. His famous beard and mustache were groomed perfectly and extended down and out in both directions. He wore the uniform of the general-in-chief with all its ribbons, sashes, and spectacle.

Margaret heard the announcement of Comtesse de Castiglione. She remembered that Jackie had mentioned to her the Comtesse was one of Empress Eugenie's closest friends, and on occasion, they would secretly attend masquerades in disguise. They wanted to attend innocuously and be able to engage with the attendees without being recognized. Many trysts occurred amongst the nobilities during the events, and there were rumors even the imperial family engaged in such activities.

"Lord Monte Robineau and Lady Jacquelyn Seandra Allantes, the Vicomtesse of Durante." Margaret watched as Jackie curtsied and Monte bowed to the emperor and empress. After a polite exchange of greetings, they moved forward towards the central Pavillion de L'Horloge, where the ball was being held.

It was their turn. "Lord Michel Robineau, the Marquis de Badour, and Lady Margaret Wellesley, the Countess of Renwick." Margaret curtsied and Michel bowed to the imperial couple.

"We are pleased to meet you, Lady Margaret, and you are welcome again, Lord Robineau."

The emperor seemed to be staring at her for an uncommon amount of time. Was it her imagination or was he showing her an excessive amount of interest?

"Thank you, Your Majesty," Margaret said.

"Your majesty does us a great honor with an invitation for this evening's festivities," Michel stated.

"The pleasure is ours. We are glad that you brought this fair lady to join us."

There it was again. He seemed to be paying an abnormal amount of attention to her. She had not heard him speak this much to any of the previous people in the processional line.

Margaret glanced over at the empress, and by the sudden dissatisfied look on her face, it did not seem she was thrilled with the attention the emperor was paying to Margaret.

"I am glad that it pleases, Your Majesty," Michel stated.

"We will see you in the ball shortly, Lord Robineau, Lady Margaret."

The interaction left Margaret perplexed. Had he been flirting with her? She had heard that he engaged in "petite distractions" with other women, but would he be so bold as to hint he would be interested in her, especially in front of the empress and the man courting her? He was the emperor; maybe he felt he could do whatever he wanted without regard for anyone else.

"I am going to need to keep my eye on you tonight. The emperor seems to be taken with you. Of course, who would blame him? You are remarkable."

Margaret blushed. She had hoped that Michel had not been aware of the emperor's apparent notice of her. She had been patiently waiting for the marquis to propose, and she did not want this to delay it from happening. What if he thought this was always going to happen? Men often were interested in her, but she was a loyal wife. She hoped he gave her the chance to prove it.

"I think you are reading more into the situation than what is actually there."

"Either way, you are going to find me hard-pressed to leave your side."

She stopped and turned to face Michel. "Do you think he has a chance with me?"

He furrowed his brows together. "Do you want him to have a chance?"

She stepped closer to Michel and replied, "Do *you* want him to have a chance?"

Michel moved forward until they were only inches apart. She could feel his breath on her face as she waited for him to respond. "No, I do not."

"Then what are you going to do about it?"

He grabbed her around the waist and pulled her into an embrace. "This," he said, as he leaned down and claimed her mouth with his own. The kiss was hesitant at first, but as she allowed it to continue, he deepened it. She let herself melt into his arms, surprised to find she wanted more of his touch.

"Did that answer your question?"

"Most assuredly."

"You have put the emperor out of your mind, then."

"Who?" she said playfully.

"Good. Keep it that way."

When they entered the ballroom, Margaret was shocked by the sheer grandeur of the room and the decadence within it. The room was gleaming with gold, marble, and crystal from the pillars to the windows to the floors.

Jackie rushed up to them. "I need to talk to you, Margaret." She glanced over at Michel and he gestured for them to go ahead. Jackie pulled her aside, saying, "I heard that the emperor was dallying with you, Margaret."

"Where did you hear that?"

"Lady Ginene was behind you a couple of groups back. She overheard everything."

Which meant that if Lady Ginene knew what had transpired, everyone else would soon enough.

"It is true, there were some mild innuendos from His Majesty, but that is not the biggest shock. The real revelation was Michel finally showed me how he feels."

"He *showed* you how he feels?"

"Not like *that*. He kissed me."

"On the cheek?"

"No, silly, on the lips."

"How was it?"

"Surprisingly, it was incredible."

"Oh, Margaret, I am so glad for you. You were so worried about your connection to the marquis."

"I know. It proved to me that we have something tangible between us and it is not simply platonic."

"This is the best news of the night, even better than my best friend catching the eye of the emperor."

Margaret rolled her eyes. "We need to be getting back to the men."

"Agreed."

They found the Robineau brothers standing near the edge of the dance floor, and they both turned to greet the women. The orchestra was tuning their instruments and the couples watched as the emperor and empress entered the room. The imperial couple made their way onto the dance floor and took their positions to start the evening celebrations. The music began and the regal couple began to follow the steps to the first dance. A few moments went by and the rest of the guests joined the emperor and empress on the dance floor.

The rest of the night was a luxurious fête, and Margaret enjoyed herself immensely. She finally felt like she could just savor being with Michel and enjoy his company rather than always wondering how he felt about her.

After several songs, she excused herself to go to the powder room and Jackie accompanied her.

"This night has been what all of us have needed. Monte and I seem to be getting along well for once, and you and Michel are finally on the same page."

"It has been a delightful evening, and I am glad that we are all here."

Looking in the mirror, Margaret reached for her clutch to apply more rouge, then remembered she left it on one of the tables. "I need to go fetch my clutch, Jackie. I will return momentarily."

As she exited the powder room and headed down the hallway towards the ballroom, she heard a somewhat familiar voice from behind her. "I had hoped to run into you all evening."

Margaret swiveled around to find the emperor standing only a few feet from her. "Good evening, Your Majesty. Why, perchance, were you seeking me out?"

"To finish our conversation, or perhaps, if I am lucky, to discuss matters less suitable in front of others," he said as he regarded her with sensual desire and licked his lips.

"I am flattered, Your Majesty, but I am afraid you are mistaken about my availability for such a discussion."

"Are you referring to Lord Robineau?"

"Yes, he is currently courting me."

He made a motion of unconcern with his hands. "I can take care of that."

"As I said, I am flattered, but that will not be necessary."

The emperor closed the distance between them. He reached out and gently stroked her cheek with his hand. "You are sure I cannot persuade you otherwise?"

"I am—"

Before she could answer the emperor, Jackie came from around the corner. "There you are, Margaret. I had wondered what was taking you so long."

Immediately, Jackie froze in place. She looked shocked to see the emperor and Margaret in such intimate proximity.

The emperor stepped back rapidly and narrowed his eyes, as if in a warning not to mention what transpired. "Good evening, ladies. We will see you back at the ball."

Both women nodded in agreement and said in unison, "Yes, Your Majesty."

Once the emperor was out of range, Jackie asked, "Did I interrupt what I think I interrupted?"

"You did. Thank you."

"He really must have taken a fancy to you to make such an effort."

"Please, do not mention it to Michel."

"I would not dream of it, chéri. What happened just now stays between you and me. Honestly, it is of little consequence. I hear he flirts with the majority of the noble women."

Margaret appreciated her friend's attempt to make light of the encounter, but it had made her feel uncomfortable and without control. She honestly did not know how she would have gotten out of the situation without offending the emperor if Jackie had not intruded.

When they came back to be with Michel and Monte in the ballroom, Margaret tried to push the incident out of her mind. She wanted to focus on her time with Michel, but she worried someone could have observed the interaction between the emperor and her. Should she tell Michel before someone else had the opportunity? She did not know which was a better option: to stay silent or to reveal what happened.

"You look pallid, Margaret. Are you feeling faint?"

Margaret avoided Michel's searching gaze. "I think I may have partaken of one too many glasses of champagne this eve. Would you mind escorting me over to one of the chairs, Michel, and allow me to rest briefly?"

"Certainly. Here, let me help you." He took her hand and wrapped it through his arm as he walked her over to the chairs.

Michel sat down next to Margaret, his hand still firmly holding hers on his other arm. He looked at her intently. "Ever since you returned from the powder room, you seem to be troubled. What is the matter?"

She felt she needed to be honest with him. She did not want to keep anything from Michel if she could help it. "When I was returning to acquire my clutch from one of the tables, the emperor stopped me in the hallway."

Margaret felt Michel stiffen. "What happened?"

"He implied that he wanted to pursue a liaison with me."

She heard him mumble a few French curse words under his breath before saying, "I realize he is the emperor, but His Majesty can be uncouth sometimes. How did you handle the situation?"

"I told him it was not an option as I was involved with you."

"Did he move on?

"Unfortunately not. He told me he could take care of it. I assume he meant he could pressure you to stop courting me."

"And?"

"And… I told him that would not be necessary." Margaret reached out and gently touched the side of Michel's face with her gloved hand. "You should know by now where my loyalties lie."

"I want to believe you, Margaret, but you always seem so elusive. I feel like there is something always unsaid between us. I sometimes wonder if you truly want to be with me or if you are allowing me to court you for the resources I possess."

Margaret flinched at the harshness of his words. It hurt to think he mistrusted her intentions. She thought they had taken steps in furthering their relationship, but this made her question all of their progress.

"I am sorry you feel that way, Michel. If you will pardon me."

She pulled free from his grasp and stood up. Without a word, she lifted her skirts and hurried towards the veranda doors beside them. She pushed through them and gulped in the fresh air.

What was she going to do? It was her own fault he felt that way. She *had* been keeping secrets from him. She did not tell Michel the truth about her scandalous past or the fact that she was searching for her brother in France. How could he feel assured in their relationship when there was tension manifesting from her keeping information from him? She knew a relationship built on secrets could not last, but she was too afraid of his reaction to tell him the truth.

"You always seem to be running away from him."

Margaret swirled around to find Pierre standing a few feet behind her.

"What are you doing out here?"

"I saw your hasty departure from the marquis and could tell from your demeanor that you were upset. I wanted to check on you, because despite everything that has transpired between us, I still care for you deeply."

"I did not even know you were coming to the emperor's ball."

"You would not. We have not been spending much time together as of late."

Margaret felt guilty over cutting Pierre so harshly out of

her life. He did not deserve the treatment she had given him, but she also could not afford to give him false hope.

"I have been otherwise involved."

"Indelibly, with the marquis, I am sure."

"Yes. We have grown closer over the past weeks."

"As evidenced by your argument just a few moments ago," he said with a hint of sarcasm.

"All couples quarrel."

"But the question is, do you want to make up with him?"

"I do."

"Do you want to because you love and desire him or because you still think he offers you the best possibility of protection?"

Margaret looked away, hating the fact that Pierre knew how her mind worked better than she did herself.

"I am going to assume, by your lack of response, that it is the latter. Why can you not see that I can protect you just as readily as the marquis can? I know you have true affection for me. You could have everything you ever wanted if you would just let yourself." He reached out and took her face in his hands. "All you have to do is pick me, Margaret. I am right here. All you have to do is say 'yes.'"

Pierre slowly leaned down and took her mouth with his own. She felt herself quiver as his body molded to her own and he wrapped his arms around her. It had been months since she had allowed herself to have physical contact with Pierre because her attraction to him superseded all her rational thoughts. She felt herself hypnotized by his lips pressed against her own and mesmerized by his hands touching her body. Margaret knew she should not give in to him—she would be compromising everything she had been working towards building—but Pierre's touch was her downfall. She wrapped her arms around his neck and leaned into his embrace.

He whispered against Margaret's lips, "Say you love me, Margaret. Say it, and I will be yours forever."

His words broke the momentary bond, and Margaret pulled away. "I cannot. I will not."

Pierre reached out for her again, but she stepped back even further. "Do not do that. It was a mistake to let it happen once. I will not let it happen again."

"You keep saying that, but here we are together."

"We are not together."

"A trivial detail you can effortlessly rectify."

"Stop it."

"Stop what?"

"Stop trying to entice me with your flirtations."

"Is it working?"

"Yes, Margaret, tell us, is it working?"

Margaret jolted and turned around to find Michel standing behind her. He looked irate to see them together in the deserted part of the imperial gardens.

"Michel, I am glad you came to find me. Shall we go inside to dance?"

"Perhaps. First, I would like to hear your answer to the vidame's question."

"It is not effective. I am committed to my courtship with you, Michel. Pierre and I were just parting ways, and I was coming back inside to find you."

Michel glared at Pierre for several seconds before saying, "You need to stop harassing Lady Margaret the way you have been. She has made her choice to allow me to court her, and you need to accept her decision."

Pierre scoffed. "Think what you will, but you do not intimidate me, and you will not tell me what to do." He softened his gaze and tone. "Until next time, Margaret." Pierre bowed and left them alone.

"He is persistent, I give him credit."

"I am sorry. He does not seem to be able to stop his conduct."

"That makes two times this evening that I have had to fight off men who were making advances towards you."

"I hope it does not persuade you from continuing to court me."

"I told you I would learn how to fight for you. I think I have made a fair attempt at it tonight."

"Indeed, you have, Michel."

"Let us go back inside. I want to dance with you and put all of this behind us."

"Agreed."

Margaret was disturbed by Michel's earlier comments when he alluded to the fact that he thought she was letting him court her for questionable reasons. She had wanted to defend herself, but the truth was she had been allowing him to pursue her to provide security for her and Henry. She had been so concerned with that one detail, she had failed to focus on all the other aspects to Michel she had grown to appreciate. If she considered how she truly felt about him, she regarded him as an engaging conversationalist over dinner, an excellent partner at cards, and a loyal companion who shared a common faith in God. He was more to her than just a means to safety, but was it enough? Could she ever love him the way she had loved Henry? And if she never found herself feeling love for him in that way, would companionship suffice?

Unsettled by the troubling questions swirling inside her, Margaret pushed her worries away for the night and allowed herself to be distracted by the surrounding entertainment. The rest of the night passed without occurrence, and Margaret poured herself into bed in the early morning hours.

CHAPTER 14

*M*ichel had offered to escort Margaret to the opera again. She had been let down when he did not propose to her at his home, but she felt a true intimacy with him for the first time because of the secret he shared with her about his sister. Added with their intimate kiss at the emperor's ball, she was confident that he planned to propose shortly.

Jackie and Monte would be attending with them per usual, and she wondered what was in store for them this evening. Jackie was the most outrageous and rash person that Margaret had ever met. But she had to admit, she liked it. She liked the freedom that she experienced when she was around Jackie. Her friend made everything so much more alive. It was astonishing how much commotion one little vivacious redhead could stir up.

She shook her head as she thought about the last ball they

had attended. It was the masked ball at the Paris Opera at Salle Le Peletier. Jackie had decided to have a mask made that had a slight but unmistakable resemblance to Lady Ginene, one of the French noble gossips, known to be the ugliest of the titled women.

Jackie had proudly marched right up to Lady Ginene, bowed with her mask high for everyone to see, and said, "My lady, you are looking exceptionally lovely tonight."

The incident created such a sensation that the gentlemen were turning red from holding in laughter and the ladies were hiding behind their masks so that their blushing was not apparent.

Monte was so embarrassed by Jackie that Margaret had been sure he was going to end their association permanently. But in the end, he laughed it off and gave her a giant kiss on the mouth for her performance.

Jackie had smirked at Margaret and said in a haughty whisper, "That will teach that old cow not to tangle with me."

Tonight was probably going to follow a similar pattern, but then it always did when Jackie was present.

Picking up the rouge from her vanity table, Margaret placed an extra dab on each cheek, as was the fashion currently. She looked at herself critically in the mirror and approved of how she looked. The teal satin gown she wore had tucks and folds, creating layers in a crescendo effect. It was complemented by cap sleeves and a bow that tied in the back. The fit accentuated her body in all the right places.

Margaret was about to leave when Sarah came around the corner with Henry in her arms.

"Would you like to say good night to him, my lady."

"Yes, thank you, Sarah."

She walked over to them and gently placed a kiss on her son's forehead. "Good night, my sweet boy. Be good for Sarah and I will see you in the morning."

Sarah took Henry and headed up the stairs to put him to sleep. Margaret grabbed her clutch and shawl as she headed out the door to the opera.

The performance of *The North Star,* in honor of the late great opera composer Giacomo Meyerbeer, had been one of the best productions she had ever seen. The main protagonist, Peter the Great, won the heart of the woman he loved with his magical flute playing, which also saved her from going insane. The narrative kept Margaret on the edge of her seat and she found herself transfixed.

But now that the opera was over, Margaret was anxious, as she suspected at any moment that Michel was going to propose to her. Jackie and Monte had left to mingle with the other box occupants across the theater.

She licked her lips subconsciously as she glanced out of the corner of her eye at the man sitting next to her. She watched him conversing with one of the barons who had stopped by their box. As usual, a parade of members of the

French upper crust had made their way through the marquis's box, and every time he would start to talk to her between acts, someone would interrupt them. It had made the night seem particularly wearisome. She just wanted it to finally be over so she could start planning their future together.

Absentmindedly, she was lightly tapping her foot in impatience. The marquis noticed her fidgeting and made his excuses. After the young Baron Olindora left their box, Michel turned to face her and said, "I have something to discuss with you."

She turned to him anxiously. "Yes?"

He took her hands in his own. "I have thought long and hard about this. You are beautiful and graceful and have been raised to be in my world. I want you to marry me."

Michel pulled out a small velvet box and opened it. Then he turned it around so she could see what was inside. She took in a deep breath as her eyes focused on the most beautiful emerald ring she had ever seen. It was exquisite, Henry's ring paling in comparison.

Pulling the ring out of the box, he took her hand between his own. Michel smiled as he removed her glove and was about to put the ring on her hand when he stopped. She glanced down and realized that, in her hasty departure, she had forgotten to take off Henry's ring.

She stared at it for a moment and froze, unable to remove it. It felt like her last connection to him. But it was time to take it off. After all, she still had her son, and he was the only connection she truly needed to remember Henry.

With a silent, deep breath, Margaret twisted the ring off her finger and put it in her skirt pocket. She then gave her shaking hand back to Michel. He slid the ring onto her finger and said, "Good, it fits." He looked her in the eyes and explained, "I was not sure it was going to fit your delicate hands since it was my grandmother's ring. She left it to me so that I could give it to my intended wife."

Margaret looked at him and waited for him to say more, to tell her he loved and wanted her because he could not live without her. She waited and the words never came. But she knew it did not matter. Marrying him was the best choice. He would give her and Henry protection from both Witherton and Catherine, not to mention financial stability beyond anything she could ever obtain on her own.

When it came down to it, love had brought her nothing but heartache, and she realized that it was highly overrated. She was willing to give up her chances to find love if it meant that Henry would be safe and secure.

She forced a smile and replied, "Michel, I accept your proposal. I will be honored to marry you."

"Splendid. I cannot wait to make you my wife." He leaned forward and placed a peck on her lips. His mouth lingered on hers for several seconds before Margaret gently pulled away.

"I cannot wait for us to be wed, Michel. I have waited so long for this moment. I am elated."

"I am pleased to hear as much. I am looking forward to starting our lives together." He leaned in, pulled her into his arms, and kissed her again, that time with passion. Margaret let him deepen the kiss as she tried to match his desire, but something was holding her back.

Margaret broke free from the kiss. "I need to take my leave for a moment. I must go powder my nose. I will only be a few moments."

Michel nodded, and Margaret gracefully stood to her feet and exited the marquis's box. She hastily went down the stairs and headed towards the ladies' room. She had done it. It was over now and she was engaged to the Marquis de Badour, one of the richest and most powerful men in France.

She looked down at the ring he had just given her. It was gorgeous, but it almost felt like a slave ring. She had sold herself to the highest bidder for security and status, and now she must reap what she had sown. She had convinced herself that, if she built up enough defenses around her, both exter-nally and internally, she would be content. She had feared Michel did not desire her as more than a companion, but that worry had been put to rest as he had been showing much affection as of late. However, her fears regarding it had been replaced by worry of whether friendship and desire could be enough to sustain a relationship. She wondered if she would ever be happy again without a man who truly loved her.

Margaret was about to turn the corner to enter the

powder room when an arm reached out from the shadows and pulled her out of vision of anyone else.

Startled, she let out a little yelp, but a quick hand closed itself over her mouth. She fought against the stranger who had a hold of her.

And then a familiar voice said, "Countess, it is I, Josef Mulchere. I am sorry about the intrusion, but I needed to speak to you immediately."

She went still and he released her from his grip. He stepped back and whispered, "I have located your brother."

Margaret spun around quickly while covering her mouth with her hand to keep from crying out in excitement. It was the dream she thought would never come true. She had hoped to hear those words for so long but never fully allowed herself to believe it would happen. Secretly, she had worried that he may have survived the initial wreck but had died from exposure or possibly from disease shortly after. But he was alive. Her brother was alive, and Henry was going to have an uncle.

"However, there is some alarming news regarding his condition. He does not remember anything from his childhood. He has complete memory loss from before the shipwreck. I checked out his story without him knowing.

"He was found by two fishermen several miles from the wreckage site. He was floating on a makeshift raft, unconscious along with another man, George Bishop, who you mentioned to me as being the only survivor. They saw your brother's fine linen pants and boots and his aristocratic features and realized he might be worth something to someone.

"They took both men, assuming they might be able to get a reward for finding them. When your brother and George regained consciousness, they became aware both men had lost their memories. They had no idea who the men were or where they came from, so they dumped them off at the docks.

"I found all of this out when I tracked down George Bishop, who still works as a fisherman but further down the coast of France. He still could not recall the details from the day of the shipwreck, but all his other memories and the ones from how they were rescued had come back to him over time.

"When they had asked him about your brother originally, he had still been injured from the wreck and everything from that time was muddled. He could not recall the conversation they had, and he was unaware that anyone was still looking for your brother. He assumed he had been found and returned home. He said he would have come forward with the details if he had known any different."

"You found out he survived the shipwreck, but how did you track him down without his memories?"

"There were rumors of a boy who had been found on the docks that matched the description of your brother. He had managed to find odd jobs, as well as, shall I say, less desirable ways of obtaining money." He looked at her pointedly.

She did not understand his meaning, asking, "What do you mean, 'less desirable'?"

"I am sorry to say, my lady, that he has been arrested several times for pickpocketing as well as... selling women services."

Margaret gasped. "Oh goodness! It never occurred to me that he might have had to do detestable things in order to survive."

"There is more."

She shook her head and replied, "I do not think I want to hear any more about what he has done." Margaret reached out her hand and placed it on the wall to steady herself.

Mulchere waited for her to give him the signal to continue. Realizing she needed to know exactly what she was dealing with, she nodded for him to go on. "He has also gained an unprofitable gambling habit, and coupled with his deep taste for the drink, it seems he has picked up a whole list of enemies as well as owed money."

Margaret tightened her lips together. It seemed that her brother, her idol, had become nothing more than a common thief and hooligan. She wondered if it was even worth trying to bring back his memories. Who was to say he could even find his way back to the brother she loved? Perhaps he went down with the ship all those years back after all. She hated thinking about the possibility that her brother was really lost to her.

Hearing all the detestable things he had done, Margaret asked, "How are you certain that it is him?"

Mulchere pulled something from his pocket that was wrapped in a handkerchief and handed it to her. Margaret gingerly opened the small package and trembled as she stared at the contents. She instantly recognized her brother's monogrammed pocketknife. He had carried it with him everywhere since the day their father gave it to him on their tenth birthday. It was also the last gift he had been given before he was lost at sea.

"How did you get this?"

"It was actually the key to finding your brother. I came across it at a shop while I was working for another client. I immediately knew it was his from the description you had given me when you went over the possible items he would have had on him when the ship went down. I asked the owner of the shop the details regarding how he came to be in possession of it. He informed me that the young man who had brought it in to sell was known around that area of town as having a dire reputation and associating with a bad element. Apparently, he had gotten into such bad debt, he was selling off the last of his possessions in order to scrape together enough money to keep the collectors at bay."

Margaret shook her head in bewilderment. There was no denying the fact that it was definitely her brother. Part of her was relieved to know he was alive, but another part was saddened by what had happened to him since his presumed death.

"What do you want to do, my lady?"

He was her brother. If nothing else, she owed it to her

father to at least try to reach him. Besides, he was heir to the Renwick title, and there had to be some part of their family left in him. She lifted her chin with pride and stated, "I plan to go to him, right now, and do whatever it takes to make him remember who he really is: Randall Thomas Wellesley, the Earl of Renwick."

Mulchere made a disapproving sound in his throat, but after a few moments said, "As you wish, my lady."

"Where can I find him?"

"He is down at one of the pubs by the docks. He frequents them quite often, but you may want to wait until morning. Not only is it unsafe for a lady to go down there at night, but I also think you should let the drink wear off before you confront him."

She shrugged off his warning. "For eight years I have waited to find my brother. I do not intend to wait another minute to talk to him. I am going to take care of this tonight. If you will excuse me, I need to go and give my leave to the marquis."

Hesitantly, he reached out and grabbed her, stopping her. She cringed slightly, the intrusive touch of men still bothering her sometimes, but he did not seem to notice.

"Then I am coming with you. I would not be able to live with myself if you met with any harm down there."

"If you insist, wait for me up the street, and I will pick you up in my carriage." She turned around and started to make her way back to the marquis's box.

Margaret hated lying to Michel. He had always been

honest with her, even when it came to why he wanted to marry her. She had beauty, grace, and a title to match his own. He never lied by saying he loved her, and she respected him for it. But she knew that, if she told him the truth, he would try to stop her or at least insist that he come with her. She needed to do this on her own, and she needed to do it this evening. She feared she might lack the courage to do so if she waited. No, tonight was the night. She was finally going to find her brother and bring him back.

"Michel, I need to take my leave, as a family situation needs to be resolved immediately."

He stood up, saying, "Then I will accompany you."

Just as Margaret feared, he wanted to come with her, and she knew she could not have him see her brother in the condition in which she would most likely find him. She felt she knew Michel and believed he would not react negatively, but part of her worried he would end their engagement if he disapproved of her brother. If she could resolve things with Randall and bring him back from the substandard way in which he was living, then she would be able to introduce them at that point.

"That will not be necessary, as it is a delicate matter." She could tell by his demeanor that his mind had not been changed by her statement, so she added, "It has to do with my son, and I think your presence at this time may only make the circumstances worse."

A hurt look came over Michel's face, and Margaret instantly felt guilty for keeping the truth from him. She hated using her son as an excuse. She tried to justify it by convincing herself what was going on affected her son since she was doing all of this to save his uncle.

"I see. I would prefer to accompany you, but if you feel this is how you need to proceed, I will yield to your wishes."

"Thank you. I will see you tomorrow, then, for brunch?"

Michel nodded in agreement, and Margaret quietly left the opera house.

CHAPTER 15

The stench of sweat and alcohol was thick in the room. Profuse enough, it made Margaret gag. She pulled out her handkerchief and daintily put it over her nose and mouth. Looking around the sparsely furnished little room, she spotted Randall. She recognized him instantly, as their physical features were almost identical. Growing up, people would call them matching bookends.

Although he was no longer the boy she remembered, she hoped a part of him was still present. Perhaps her brother was deep down inside, and with some help, he could be rescued from the mess of a man that she saw sitting across the tavern from her now.

Randall had his head thrown back, laughing with his arm swung around the waist of one of the tavern's servers. The wench leaned forward and said something to her brother that Margaret thankfully could not understand. He winked at the woman and then slapped her on the bottom. The girl rewarded him with a big kiss on the mouth and then went to go refill his drink.

Margaret, followed closely by Mulchere, made her way to Randall's side. She stopped only a few feet away, and at first, he did not notice her standing there. Then as if he sensed her, he glanced up, his eyes growing wide with surprise, then disdain.

"If you are here for a night on the wild side with a local seaman, I am not for sale."

She gasped and raised her hand to slap him but thought better of it. She did not want things to start out like that. Instead, she replied, "That is not why I am here, sir."

He laughed, then asked, "Why, then, my dear, would a fine lady like you be careless enough to come down here, especially at this time of night?" Then he licked his lips in a lecherous manner. "Perhaps I will take it upon myself to sample the goods." He reached out to grab her, but Mulchere stepped in as her protector and pushed him back into his chair.

"Who is that?"

Margaret ignored his question and said, "I came here because I have information about your past."

He raised an eyebrow, then shrugged. "Lady, my past is of no concern to me… and whatever your interest is, I do not care."

She glared at him for a moment before deciding to change tactics. With finesse, she said, "But I only thought that, if you were who I thought you were, you would like to know that you are exceedingly wealthy."

It was not quite a lie. Soon, he would be brother to the Marchioness du Badour, and with her new title they would be set for life. There was also the fact that he would regain the title of Earl of Renwick, and he could use it, along with all of its privileges, to create his own wealth.

That time, he looked at her with an eyebrow raised. "You do not say? So, if I am to believe any of this nonsense, tell me, how did you come to find this out?"

Margaret sighed, already exasperated by his obnoxious behavior. Randall always had a skeptical nature, constantly questioning everything and everyone. He may have lost his memories, but it seemed some of his personality was still intact.

"I know your sister, who is the Countess of Renwick and the fiancée of the Marquis de Badour. She told me she was looking for you, but I wanted to see for myself if you could be her brother before I informed her that you had been located."

Not wanting to reveal that she was actually his sister until she was certain he would believe her, she kept the information to herself. She was afraid it might cause more problems than good. And there was always the possibility that he would reject everything she said. If that happened, it would be much easier to deal with if she was detached, and this was the only way she could guarantee that.

Margaret stared at him for a few moments, taking in the

sight she never thought she would see again. It was incredible to see him after all these years. Of course, he had changed from the boy he had been at ten, but his overall features remained the same. His black hair was longer than before and hung to just above his shoulders. He did not seem to care to keep it neat any longer, as it was slicked back with grease. His body had filled out and matured into a man's physique. But his dark violet eyes and mannerisms were still so much like her own.

She wondered why he did not recognize her even on some deeper level or why he could not see the resemblance between them. Then she realized he was probably too drunk to even recognize himself.

"If I am to believe what you are saying, who am I, then?"

"Randall Thomas Wellesley, the Earl of Renwick."

"My, that is a mouthful."

"I think you should come back to my residence so that you can sleep off your inebriated state. Then in the morning, we will discuss your future."

He laughed and shook his head. "I would not mind going back to your place, but sleeping will be the last thing I want to do with you around," Randall slurred as he winked at her.

Despite her anger, she refrained from making a sharp retort that he was acting like a complete imbecile. Her brother was in no condition to be reprimanded, and she did not want to make things more difficult than they were already turning out to be. Instead, she replied, "I think sleep is exactly what you need at the moment."

"Lady, what I plan to do is play a few more hands of poker, get even more drunk, then find me a woman and take full advantage of both."

He stood up, wobbling a bit in the process, and slurred out a list of explicit words after he stumbled backwards.

"But first, I need to go to my room so I can relieve myself." He pulled down on the edge of his tattered jacket and started to stagger towards the stairs.

Mulchere leaned forward and whispered, "Perhaps we should come back in the morning and try this again."

Margaret watched the retreating figure of her brother and felt despair, realizing he really was lost to her. It hurt. It hurt more than when he had been presumably lost at sea because he was choosing to walk away. It might have been better if she had believed the sea had claimed her brother rather than see him this way.

Feeling faint, she started to sway. Then, all of a sudden, the ground started to give beneath her and she was falling backwards.

Luckily, Mulchere was directly behind her. He caught her and said, "Lady Margaret, are you all right?"

Her brother stopped as he was ascending the stairs. He pivoted around, almost falling down them in the process, and stared at them for several seconds before half stumbling over to where they were.

Margaret regained her composure and stood up as Randall narrowed his eyes at her. She lifted her chin as he watched her for several seconds before saying, "I do not know why, but when he called you by your name, it triggered something." He furrowed his eyebrows. "It was as if a fleeting image raced across my mind just for a moment."

She tightened her lips, a habit she did without even thinking about it, and his eyes grew round with shock.

"Either the drink has really gotten to me this time or I swear that I do recognize you."

A wave of happiness flooded her as she realized that perhaps it was not too late to bring her brother back from his memory loss.

"Truly?" she said hopefully. "You know who I am?"

Puzzled, he shook his head and slurred out, "No, I do not know who you are, but I do know that somehow I recognize you."

Margaret's shoulders visibly slumped forward but she pushed them back, reminding herself that at least it was a start. "I am glad that I seem familiar. It encourages me, enough in fact to ask you again if you will come as a guest to my home."

Frowning, he weighed his decisions, and for a fraction of a moment, Margaret feared she was going to have to face his rejection again. But instead, he shrugged and said casually, "I suppose I have nothing keeping me here…. And you say that I am rich?"

She nodded. Whatever it took to keep him interested.

"Just allow me to go upstairs and grab my belongings."

Looking him up and down, she doubted he had anything upstairs that he would need once he was reinstated as the

Earl of Renwick. But that was selfish of her to discount the last eight years of his life.

"I will wait outside in my carriage. But hurry. It is time for you to leave this part of your life behind."

He raised an eyebrow at her and said, "I hope you know what you're getting yourself into."

She smiled. "I am willing to take on the challenge."

Randall tilted his head to the side. "You know, that sounds a lot like something I would say. I think we might just get along, Lady Margaret." With that, Randall turned around and headed up the stairs to his room.

Margaret quickly headed towards the exit. She could not wait to get away from the detestable place that reeked of so many repugnant things. She hoped her brother could leave all of this behind him. Part of her worried that he had gotten used to living this way, that he would prefer it to the life he had been born to live. What if he did not want to live a life of a nobleman?

As she left the tavern, Margaret was lost in thought of how she was going to go about helping her brother regain his memories. But as she approached her carriage, she felt a shiver climb up her back. Something was not right with her surroundings, but she could not quite discern what was out of place. She slowly scanned the area around her, trying to pinpoint what was making her feel uneasy.

From behind her, she heard an odd noise, almost like feet shuffling and a loud thud. Margaret swiftly turned around and gasped when she saw Mulchere slumped in a pile by the tavern wall. He was not moving, and she started to rush to his side, but an arm quickly wrapped around her waist while another hand covered her mouth. The stranger roughly yanked her harshly against his steely frame.

She tried to scream, but the hand over her mouth muffled her efforts, and no amount of struggle was helping her escape her captor.

Margaret heard her carriage driver yell from behind her, "Unhand Lady Margaret at once."

As she was being dragged away from her carriage, she saw her driver knocked out by two additional accomplices and left on the side of the street.

Suddenly, something dark draped over her eyes, and she realized a bag had been placed over her head. Margaret began to panic. She had no idea what was happening, but she knew that if she did not get away somehow, she was never going to see her son again.

She began to thrash even more, frantic to free herself, but to no avail. In an instant, she felt herself being lifted into what she could only assume was another carriage. Then a second set of hands grabbed her and pulled her close.

"Don't fight me, girl. If you do, it will go much harder for you." The voice was deep, scratchy, and thick with an accent from the poorest area of the city. Margaret acknowledged the ominous tone in his voice and went absolutely still.

"That's better. You don't want to make me angry."

She felt the carriage shudder, and hastily they lurched forward. Margaret tried to keep track of the turns they made and keep a count between them, but the disorientation from being blind from the bag over her head made it impossible for her to do so. She realized that there was no way she would be able to know where she was once she arrived wherever they were taking her.

Focusing on fighting down the fear that was continuously building inside her, Margaret tried to remain calm. She had to get her emotions under control if she was going to survive whatever was happening to her.

After some time passed, she felt the carriage come to a halt. Then she was lifted down and passed to another stranger who roughly placed her over his shoulder. She heard a door open, and as they entered, she felt an abrupt burst of heat and could smell the faint scent of hot metal and ash.

Callously, Margaret was dropped into a chair, and she could hear heavy breathing very close. Seconds ticked by with only the stranger's breathing to keep her company.

Margaret sat motionless with her hands clenched in her lap, afraid that any movement on her part might make the stranger think she was trying to escape.

And though the idea had crossed her mind to try to make a break for it, she knew the stranger was probably faster and most definitely knew the layout of where she was being held. He would no doubt be able to catch her before she could make it to the door. If she bolted, all she would succeed in doing was making the stranger exceptionally livid. Her only choice was to wait and hope she found a better opportunity to get away.

She heard what sounded like a chair scraping the ground, and the heavy breathing came even closer. It penetrated the bag over her head and she inhaled sharply, waiting to see what the stranger had planned for her.

Unexpectedly, the bag was ripped from Margaret's head and bright light assaulted her eyes from the nearby fire. She squinted and tried to establish her surrounding, but it took several moments for her eyes to be able to focus. She took a deep breath and held it when she found herself only inches from a man with dark skin and intense black eyes. He was bent down so he could look directly into her eyes. She wanted to flinch and turn away from his gaze, but something made her stare right back at him.

"I don't want to tie you to the chair, but if you do anything besides sit there, I will make you very uncomfortable."

Margaret immediately recognized the voice as the stranger from the carriage.

"Do you understand me, girl."

From his tone, she could tell he was making a statement, not asking a question, but she found herself nodding to affirm that she did indeed understand the implication from being made "very uncomfortable."

"You're probably wondering why you were brought here."

Margaret nodded again, still too afraid to do anything more than that.

"I was commissioned to find a young woman fitting your description who has something my employer wants. Do you know what I'm talking about?"

Margaret licked her lips and slowly shook her head.

The man stood up and slowly walked behind her, placing his hands on both of her shoulders. He tightened his grip, just enough pressure to make Margaret feel a sharp pain shoot through her body.

"I think you should rethink your last answer. It took a great deal of work to find you, but I'm under the notion that you're the girl my employer is looking for. The only reason I haven't delivered you to my employer yet is that he doesn't take kindly to having his time wasted, and if you aren't who I think you are, I'm not willing to risk his wrath by delivering the wrong girl."

The man continued to walk around Margaret until he came full circle to stand in front of her again. He reached behind him and pulled the chair to him, then sat down, never taking his eyes off Margaret.

He leaned forward and whispered in a hard voice, "So, we're going to stay here until I'm absolutely certain that you are who I think you are."

The panic Margaret had been pushing down was beginning to bubble up. She knew the employer he talked about must be Witherton, since only he would be despicable enough to hire someone capable of kidnapping and threatening her. He had it done to her before back in England, and it was exactly the type of move he would make again.

With a shaky voice, Margaret asked, "What is it that your employer wants exactly? I have nothing of any value as my family was destitute before I came to France."

"What my employer wants does not have a monetary worth."

"What do you mean? What is he after?"

"He wants what you took from him."

"I do not know what you mean. I have not taken anything from anyone. I think you are ill-advised in who you think I am."

The stranger lunged forward, slamming his hands down on either side of the chair Margaret sat in.

He spat out, "Don't lie to me, girl. We both know what you took from my employer, and he will get back what's his, no matter what it takes."

That time, Margaret could not keep herself from flinching. She quickly turned away from the stranger to conceal her distress.

She insisted, "I am sorry, but you have the wrong person. I know it is not what you want to hear, but it is the truth."

With only inches between them, he forcefully grabbed Margaret's face and made her look at him. "Everyone has been advised that you left France, but I had a hunch that it might not be true. So, I stayed around and continued to search here while everyone else moved on to other areas. I was about to give up myself when I received information that a young English noblewoman fitting the description of the girl I was hired to find was living amongst the aristocrats here in France. So, I started to watch you. I've been watching you for days now, your comings and goings, and I am very, very good at my job."

"Please, I have not done anything to deserve this."

The stranger leaned back in his chair and shrugged. "Not my problem. I don't involve myself in the personal aspects of a situation. I just do what I'm paid to do."

"You have to let me go. I have a family, a child who depends on me."

He narrowed his eyes and stated with a hint of veiled implication, "I am aware of your son. It's one of the main reasons I believe you to be the girl I'm searching for."

Margaret blanched at the remark. Was this stranger interested in her son because Catherine found her? Did Witherton know she had a child? If he did, God help her and Henry because her worst fears were now realized. The duke would stop at nothing to take him from her.

Adamantly, she stated, "My son has nothing to do with this."

"He has everything to do with this."

"You are mistaken."

"I don't make mistakes."

The stranger stood up and crossed his arms. He stared at her for several moments before saying, "I'm going to let you think on what we've talked about. When I come back, you better hope your answers satisfy me."

With that, the man turned away and left the room through a side door.

Margaret looked at her surroundings for the first time. The room's walls were made of old grey rock, and the only door she could see was the one the stranger had just walked through. There was a fire in a round pit in the center of the room, which made Margaret think that the place may have been a blacksmith shop at one time. But besides the two chairs, it seemed that the room had been stripped of anything else. Apparently, the stranger had prepared the area by making sure to leave nothing that would aid in her escape.

What was she going to do? Her worst fear was coming true. Witherton had found her and she was going to lose her son and possibly her life as well. Of course, without her son, she would not have a life anyway. She would rather be dead than live without him. But what scared her most was the thought of what would happen to Henry if the duke was able to get a hold of him. That monster was incapable of raising a child, let alone one who was illegitimate. And what if he came to the realization that he was not his son at all and decided to get rid of him because he was Henry's child? Margaret had to do something. She had to get free for the sake of her son!

Hearing a faint noise from behind her, she jumped up and spun around but saw nothing at first. But as she looked more closely, she could make out a distant shape in the shadows. Margaret whispered, "Who's there?"

From out of the shadows, her brother emerged with one finger raised to his mouth, silencing her reaction. Quickly, he grabbed her around the shoulders and guided her towards a door that she had not been aware was behind her.

"You have to be careful. There is a man in the other room who is holding me captive. I think he has an accomplice as well."

"I took care of the accomplice. The man who was in here with you did not lock the back door good enough to keep me out."

"How did you find me?"

"When I came outside to go with you, I found the man who came into the tavern with you, as well as your driver, knocked out. I was lucky enough to see the abductor's carriage pull away and followed at a distance, using your carriage. But I had to wait for the right time to be able to come in here and get you. I am sorry it took me so long."

"I am just glad that you found me."

Margaret marveled at how capable her brother appeared to be in this situation, especially after how inebriated he had been at the tavern. She assumed he must have had practice functioning in dangerous circumstances while intoxicated, given his way of life over the past several years.

"I do not know why, but I have this deep desire to want to protect you. I have never felt that way about anyone that I can remember."

She smiled at her brother. "There's a good reason for that, Randall. It is because—"

But before Margaret could reveal that they were twins, the stranger burst into the room.

"What do you think you're doing with her?"

Randall whispered to Margaret, "Get behind me."

Margaret quickly complied.

"You made the wrong choice getting involved in this, boy."

"I think you made the wrong choice by taking this woman against her will."

"Well, since I have this"—the stranger lifted his pistol and pointed it at Randall—"I think that makes any choice I make the right one."

Margaret was pressed against Randall's back, and she felt something hard and metallic against her hands. Quietly, she pulled free the pistol that Randall had hidden in his waistband. She gently placed the gun behind her back, gripping it tightly.

"Boy, I want you to move towards me. I don't want to accidently hurt the girl."

"Do not do it, Randall."

"It is all right, Margaret." Gently, Randall started to push Margaret away as he looked at her. It was as if they were children again, and she knew without either of them having to say a word what she was supposed to do.

Without warning, Randall dove onto the ground and away from Margaret as she quickly leveled the pistol at the stranger and pulled the trigger.

As the bullet struck the man, he crumpled to the ground. Margaret stood still for several seconds before she could move. Randall was promptly back on his feet and headed over to the stranger, and Margaret followed behind him.

Randall kicked the pistol away from the man's body.

There was a gurgling sound coming from the stranger's throat, and Margaret realized that he was choking on his own blood.

But even as he lay dying, the man was unable to go quietly and without threats. "I won't be the last, girl." He coughed raggedly a couple of times, and then added, "He'll send others." And then the stranger was dead.

Margaret stared at him for several moments before she started to shake. The blood that was quickly spreading across his chest made her queasy. She had to choke back the bile that was rising in her throat. She had never taken a life before. Given the opportunity, she thought she would have gladly ended Witherton's life, but now, she was not so sure. This man planned to harm her and her family, but even knowing that, the overwhelming guilt she felt was crashing in on her.

Dropping to her knees besides the man, Margaret began to sob into her hands with her head bowed in sorrow.

Randall grabbed her by the arm and pulled her up, saying, "Listen to me, Margaret. This was not your fault. You had no choice. He was going to kill me and do God knows what to you."

"I killed him. He was alive, and now he is dead because of me."

"No, Margaret, he is dead because of himself and what he chose to do."

Randall quickly looked around the room. "We need to get out of here. The other man could wake up at any time, and we do not want to be here when he does."

Margaret minutely nodded.

"Are you going to be all right?" Randall asked.

"I do not know."

"You are going to get past this. You are strong enough. I can see that."

Margaret looked at her brother for several seconds before leaning into him for support. "Take me out of this place. I cannot stand to be here another moment."

As they headed towards the door, the other man stumbled in to the room. He looked around and saw his dead boss. "What did you fools do? This isn't going to end well for you."

"You need to let us go or it is not going to end well for you," Randall stated firmly.

"Are you threatening me, kid?"

"No, I am telling you that, for anything you have done, I have done worse. You do not want to underestimate me."

The other man snorted while raising his gun and aiming it at Randall. "Your kind has no idea how the real world works."

Randall shook his head. "I think you are mistaken about what type of person I am. I am not from her pampered, noble world. I am from the same world as you, and you have no idea what I am capable of."

Margaret watched as Randall simultaneously raised his pistol and fired. The bullet hit the other man in the forehead and he fell to the ground, instantly dead. It seemed that Randall was still the same crack shot he was from childhood hunts back in England.

What shocked Margaret was that he did it so methodically, like he had shot someone before, most likely several times, and it no longer seemed to disturb him. Somehow, it seemed that Mulchere did not find out all the details of Randall's seedy past.

"I need to get you out of here before someone comes to investigate those shots."

Still shaken, Margaret did not protest as Randall guided her out of the building.

CHAPTER 16

*R*eturning to the tavern, the twins checked on how Mulchere and the carriage driver were doing after the incident. Both insisted they were unharmed other than a few bumps and bruises. The driver maintained he was well enough to drive Margaret and Randall back to her home.

As they pulled in front of her residence, Randall asked in disbelief, "This is your place?"

Margaret nodded. Still numb from the ordeal that had just happened, she stared out the carriage window as if seeing someone else's life. She had never really thought about where she lived, but she supposed that it was way above the average French society standards. If she was honest with herself, her estate was quite lavish. It had the refined older French style that many other estates tried to imitate but could not accomplish.

The two of them sat in her carriage, looking at her estate, both of them seemingly still in shock over what had transpired that night.

"I had no idea that you had *this* kind of money."

"I do not. A family friend procured this place for me. It is only temporary until I am married."

"So, you are engaged."

"I am."

"Can I ask why your fiancé did not accompany you tonight when you came to find me?"

"He offered. I did not want to involve him in this."

Randall stepped down from the carriage and then helped Margaret down as well. They were now standing outside the front doors to her estate.

"When are you going to clue me in to what happened tonight?"

Margaret glanced down at the ground, afraid that if her twin was looking her in the eyes, she would not be able to lie to him.

"They took me to ransom me back to my fiancé."

"Does this sort of thing happen often?"

"Not often, but it does happen."

"But that does not make sense, Margaret. That man said he would not be the last, that *he* will send others. The way he said 'he' seemed to imply that this person who sent him knew you somehow."

"I think it is because it has something to do with a vendetta between my fiancé and someone he knows."

"I see." But she could tell from his tone that Randall was not completely convinced she was telling him the whole truth.

Margaret looked up and wearily smiled at her brother. "I want to thank you for what you did tonight. Although, I feel as if 'thank you' does not adequately do justice for your intervention."

Randall smiled back at her. "Well, I hoped to impress you. Did it work?"

"Yes, and then some."

"Good, then maybe I can convince you dump your fiancé and run off with me."

Margaret laughed and said, "I think you are better off finding a woman more suitable for you than me."

He tenderly put his hand on the side of her face and declared, "I do believe that every woman would pale in comparison to you."

She blushed. It felt odd letting her brother continue to not know they were related. If he did, she doubted he would be making those types of comments to her. But then, it made sense that he would think her beautiful. They were twins, and even though opposite sex twins often did not look identical, they did. When she looked at him, it was like looking at a male version of herself.

"I need to tell you something—"

But before she could tell Randall that he was her brother, she heard a voice from behind her say, "Excuse me, sir, but please remove your hand from my intended."

Margaret's brother glanced up and narrowed his eyes. Then, as if he was daring the other man to start something, he slid his hand from her cheek to around her waist.

She nudged him in the side and whispered out of the corner of her mouth, "What are you doing?"

He whispered back, "Seeing if this man is worthy of you."

This was so like her brother. He had always been reckless and constantly overstepped his boundaries. Not to mention completely overprotective of her.

She stepped out of his grasp and walked over to her fiancé, saying, "Michel, I need to talk to you, privately."

The marquis glanced over at Margaret's brother skeptically and then nodded in agreement.

She pulled him aside, and when she was sure she was out of hearing of Randall, she explained, "This is not what it appears to be. That man standing on the steps to my home is my twin brother."

Michel glanced over her shoulder as if studying the other man to confirm her story. "I was under the impression that you had no family besides your son."

"That was because, until recently, my brother had been presumed dead. The ship that was supposed to bring him home from boarding school went down just off the French shoreline eight years ago. They found my brother's tattered monogrammed shirt and informed us that he had not survived. But I always had my doubts and believed that, without a body, there was a chance that he had survived.

When I left England, I decided to come here to search for him."

She waited anxiously to see what Michel planned to do. "You are informing me that you had a twin brother who has been lost all these years and this is him?"

"Yes, and I am asking you not to tell him who I am or who you are at the moment. I need time for him to adjust to everything and who he is before I give him even more information to absorb. You see, he lost his memories from before the wreck. He does not know who I am at present."

He thought for a moment. "All right. I will not say anything so long as he does not touch you like *that* again." He glanced at Margaret's brother and back at her, adding, "After what you told me, it is quite obvious, since he looks exactly like you."

She smiled and leaned up, giving him a kiss on the cheek. "Thank you for understanding."

Michel walked over to where Margaret's brother was standing. He extended his hand and Randall stared at it a moment, then slowly shook it.

"My fiancée just informed me of who you are, and I am… pleased to make your acquaintance. I know your sister quite well, and she is a very special woman."

Without acknowledging the marquis's statement, Randall asked Margaret, "Speaking of my newly acquired sister, when is it that I am going to meet her?"

Margaret stepped forward, saying, "Shortly. First, I am to

prepare you for everything that is to come, and hopefully by then, you will remember your past."

He looked at her skeptically, as if that was doubtful, but somehow she knew it was not. She was going to get her brother back. She did not come to France and go through what she had that night for nothing.

"Let us all go inside, shall we?"

Margaret rapped the door knocker. Only a few moments lapsed before Albert opened the doors, saying, "Welcome home, my lady," expecting only to find Margaret and Michel on the other side. But as he looked at the man standing next to her, his mouth gaped open, shocked to see his long-lost master, whom he had presumed dead, standing before him, quite alive.

Answering quickly before he could say anything, Margaret said, "Thank you, Albert, and could you please have the servants assembled in a half hour. I need to speak to all of them immediately."

Margaret knew she needed to explain to her servants that she had found Randall, and she wanted to do it before they had a chance to unknowingly blurt out that she was his sister.

"Yes, my lady, I will do that right now," he said, still gawking at Randall.

A sharp noise was heard down the hall, followed by the commotion of shuffling feet. There were a couple of shouts before she heard a loud yelp, and from around the corner came her son. He was rushing towards her, stumbling a little bit, as toddlers often did, and cried, "Mama."

She got down on her knees and stretched out her arms to her son. He rushed into them and she gave him a big kiss on the forehead.

It felt so good to hold him after all she had gone through that night. The thought that she might never see him again or that he could have been taken from her was still fresh.

"How's my boy?"

Henry wrinkled his nose. He was still too young to understand her. He could say "mama" and "ja-ja," which was his name for Jackie.

He had only been walking the past month, but he was a fast learner. He was keeping Sarah and Motty busy.

Wiggling out of her arms, he placed both of his hands in her hair. He loved playing with her curls. When she shook her ringlets in his face, he began to giggle and clap his hands.

"You have a son?" Randall sighed. "More and more surprises. And where might the father be?"

Margaret had temporarily forgotten about her brother. She stood and picked up Henry to face Randall.

"I was married to his father, if that was what you were wondering, but he died two years ago."

Motty rushed into the room, saying, "I am sorry, my lady. He would not go to bed without kissing you first. I can take him now if you like."

"Thank you, Motty. I would appreciate that."

The young girl took Henry and rushed out of the room with him.

"How many other surprises do you have hiding around here?"

"More than most people, I suppose." She opened the doors to her parlor and asked, "Would you both come in and join me for a nightcap?"

Wearily, Michel declined. "I need to be on my way. I just wanted to make sure your situation had been resolved without difficulty, and it seems that it has," he said, looking directly at Randall.

Margaret nodded. "Very well. Will you come by tomorrow for tea in the afternoon?"

"I will try to make it. If not, I will still be here for dinner as we planned." With that, he exited the room.

"That was quite an interesting move for your fiancé to make, leaving us alone."

She shrugged off his comment. "He trusts me."

"It is not you but me I thought he would not trust."

"Why? He has no reason to mistrust you," she said as she picked up a bottle of brandy to pour them drinks.

"No, not yet."

She did not like the sound of that. She decided that she needed to make a few things clear.

Margaret put down the bottle and said, "Let me make this plain. Nothing is going to happen between us. I need you to be aware that if you do attempt anything, you will come to regret it. Do I make myself understood?"

"I understand what you are saying. It does not mean I have to agree with it."

"Randall, I am serious."

"Fine. Let us table this discussion for another time, but in the meantime, I have another question about what happened tonight."

Margaret sighed. She was getting tired of answering questions, especially because it was a significant endeavor to keep Randall from figuring out she was lying, since they were so much alike.

"What is it?"

"If you were taken ransom because of your fiancé, why did you not tell him what happened when he showed up tonight?"

"I plan to, but I felt it warranted a longer conversation than I felt I could muster tonight. I was entirely too exhausted to get into the details."

"Why does it seem like you are keeping something from me?"

"I am not. Can you not see it is difficult for me to talk about?"

"Then I will not bring it up again."

"I appreciate it."

He walked over to the window, folded his arms across his chest, and leaned on his side to stare out.

The hair on the back of her neck started to rise. He did not know it but he was standing there and staring out the window exactly how she had back home when he had been presumably lost at sea.

"Why are you doing that?"

He turned to face her. "Doing what?"

"Looking out the window like that."

"The window back at my room at the tavern does not have this grand a view, but it does have a view of the docks that is not altogether shabby. When I need to think about something or am contemplating what I should do next, I always find comfort looking out at the world."

She tightened her lips. Any doubt she had about him being her brother was gone now. This one confession made it perfectly clear that he was Randall.

"I need to tell you something."

"Can it wait until tomorrow? I am suddenly really tired."

Margaret started to object but realized that it could wait until then. They had forever to catch up.

"Yes, it can. I will have Albert show you to your room."

After Randall turned in for the evening, Margaret addressed the servants in the salon.

"I want all of you to hear from me how my twin brother, Lord Randall Wellesley, the Earl of Renwick, was found. Most of you did not know him, with the exception of Alfred. We did not speak of my brother often, as it was a difficult subject for the family, and my father did not cope well with Randall's presumed death.

"Eight years ago, he had been returning from boarding school when the ship went down in a storm off the coast of France. Randall was never found and was presumed dead.

They never found his body, and I believed there was a chance he was still alive. When I decided to leave England, I chose to come here in hopes of finding him.

"I hired a private investigator, and he was able to locate Randall. I went to where he had been staying to bring him to stay with me. Unfortunately, he has lost his memories from before the wreck, but I am hopeful that, with time, he will regain some of them. Are there any questions?"

Alfred hesitantly asked, "From his attire, I can only assume Lord Randall was living below the standard to which his title dictates."

"Yes, Alfred, Randall faced extreme difficulties while living in France without his family. He had to make a lot of hard choices in order to survive. But all of that is in the past. We are moving forward together, and our goal is to do whatever it takes to help his memories return and to reacquaint him with the customs and privileges of his title. I have not divulged to him that I am his sister, as I did not want to overwhelm him with that information while he is adjusting. I would appreciate everyone refraining from telling him until I deem it time."

All of the servants nodded.

"That will be all. I appreciate all of your support through this process."

After the servants left the room, Margaret went over to the window and looked out at the street, which was illuminated by the gas lamps that lined it. There was a thin fog in the air, giving a mysterious feel to the view.

Margaret was grateful that she had found Randall, but she worried about his ability to adapt. Could he change in order to fit into aristocratic society? He had lived the past decade without any scrutiny or accountability. Would he be willing to give up his vagabond ways in order to live a life of privilege?

Lord, please help Randall to remember who he was and who he can be. Be with him while he learns to navigate all the changes that lay ahead for him. Help me to know the right time to tell him who I am. I want us to be close again, but I know it can only happen after I tell him I am his sister. I pray for your guidance and strength to know what to do and how to make the right decisions.

It was time to go to sleep. She was exhausted from all the activity that evening. She went from being proposed to by Michel, to finding her long-lost brother, to being kidnapped. Margaret was shocked she was still on her feet, considering. Tomorrow was a new day, and she knew she needed to rest so she would be ready to help her brother.

CHAPTER 17

The day after her abduction, Margaret was sitting in her study across from Mulchere.

"My lady, I am glad to see that you are all right, considering your ordeal from last night."

Looking at the detective, Margaret noticed the deep purple bruises on his face from being knocked out by the thugs who had taken her.

"You seem to be the one worse for wear because of last night."

"Unfortunately, it is a regrettable aspect of this type of work."

"Were you able to ascertain if my safety in France has been compromised? How many of them were there?"

"It seems there were three men working in conjunction together. The two who were killed last night and a third man

I subdued when I went back to the scene shortly after you and your brother left the tavern."

"How did you find out where we were?"

"Your brother had one of the boys who hangs outside the tavern go with him, and once the mercenaries took you inside, he sent the boy back to get me."

Her brother was quite smart. Without knowing it, he probably saved both her life and Henry's as well.

"Were you able to keep them from telling my location to who hired them?"

Mulchere paused for a moment, most likely uncomfortable talking about such a gauche subject with a lady.

"Come now, Monsieur Mulchere. When I hired you, I made it clear that you were to discuss my situation with me as if I were a man. I need you to be blunt."

Reluctantly, he continued, "I was unable to get any information from the man and was forced to bring in, shall we say, an *expert* in extracting information."

Margaret paused for a moment, thinking about what he was trying to imply. Then she realized what he meant and stated candidly, "You had him tortured."

"It was a necessary precaution."

"And what did you find out?"

"It seems the one you killed was in charge and the only one to have direct knowledge of the task. The other two men had been hired by him and were following basic instructions. He most likely did not want them to have details, fearing a double cross. I was able to find contact information for the employer on the body of the dead one. I am having false information relayed back to the employer that the woman they had been looking into was not the woman he was searching for."

"Thank you, Monsieur Mulchere."

"You are welcome, my lady."

"What happened with the third man?"

"He succumbed to his wounds and is no longer with us."

"I need to ask you one more question, and it is of the utmost importance." Margaret steeled herself for the answer. "Who hired them?"

"My lady, it was as you feared. He was hired by the Duke of Witherton."

Margaret tried not to react visibly, but inside she was filled with terror. He had almost found her. And she knew he would not stop hunting her down if he thought there was even a chance that Henry was his son.

"He cannot keep looking for me in France or he *will* find me. He must be convinced that it is useless to keep searching for me here. I have too much at stake to leave now."

"My lady, now that we know it is the duke looking for you, we can have my emissaries relay misinformation to his people directly. I will even have one of them gain employment from him to keep track of his investigation into your whereabouts."

"Will it work?"

"It should. I will do whatever it takes to make sure you are safe, my lady."

"If it does not, I will have to leave France quickly."

"My lady, I will do whatever it takes to keep you safe."

"I appreciate that—"

All of a sudden, Jackie burst into the room and cut off Margaret and Mulchere's conversation. She stood with her hands on her hips and glared at Margaret. "Why did you never tell me that you had a brother? I am your best friend, and I find out from Monte today that the marquis met him last night. I could not believe my ears. All this time, I thought you told me everything, but no, you must not, for I have come to find out this secret of yours from the lips of someone else. I felt such a fool as he looked to me to fill him in on what was going on. How could I, when you have been keeping it from me?"

Jackie's French accent always got thicker when she was upset. Absentmindedly, she shoved several of her fiery locks out of her face.

For the first time, Jackie noticed the man sitting in the room with Margaret. Slightly embarrassed but trying to mask it with a lackadaisical attitude, Jackie said flippantly, "I did not realize you had a guest. This is not your brother, is it?"

"No, it is someone who is working with me on a project, and he was just leaving," Margaret said.

Mulchere took his cue to leave. "Good day, my ladies."

"Good day, Monsieur Mulchere," Margaret replied.

Once the two women were left alone, Margaret stood up

and said to Jackie, "I was going to tell you, but I only found out yesterday that he had been located."

Pierre walked into the room. "I am sorry about my cousin, Margaret. She rushed to get ahead of me, and I was unable to keep her from bombarding you."

Jackie made an exaggerated sigh and then stated, "Well, she could have told me she was looking for him. She told you after all."

"She needed my help to find him. I am sure that, if she did not, she would not have involved me either."

"Both of you, stop it. Jackie, I am sorry if I hurt your feelings."

"I am capable of keeping a secret if I need to, Margaret." Jackie was starting to calm down. That was good. Margaret did not need her to cause a scene and draw any attention to their conversation.

"What is all the yelling about?" Randall entered the room and looked at Margaret.

Too late.

"Nothing, two of my close friends just dropped by for a visit. I did not expect you up so soon after last night."

Randall smirked. "I always recover quickly from my drinking binges." He turned and looked at Jackie and Pierre, noticing them for the first time. She could tell he was trying to minimize what happened the night before, and frankly, she was glad. She did not want to discuss it, and she definitely did not want Jackie or Pierre to know about it. She could not handle any more prodding questions about her past, not with her nerves frayed the way they were at the moment.

Jackie curtsied and extended her hand to Randall. "I am the Vicomtesse of Durante. I am... pleased to make your acquaintance."

Margaret immediately recognized the change in Jackie's voice from friendly to flirtatious.

Randall bowed and took Jackie's hand as he came up. He kissed the top of it, saying, "I am told"—he glanced at Margaret—"that I am the Earl of Renwick. I am delighted to meet such a beautiful and striking lady."

Margaret made note that even though he chose not to show it the night before, her brother was capable of demonstrating manners. Some things were like second nature if you were raised to do them your whole life. He may not remember who he was, but he did seem to remember how to act the part.

Pierre stood in the corner of the room, observing but not saying a word. He looked pale, as if seeing a ghost.

Jackie curled her lips with a suggestive smile and gave Randall a look with a deeper meaning. "I hope the countess allows us to get to know each other better." She glanced at Margaret and asked, "Would you mind, Margaret, if I got to know your brother better?"

Margaret gasped. She had not expected for Jackie to say anything, let alone blurt out her identity so quickly. But then, she supposed that Jackie did not know she had not told Randall yet.

He dropped Jackie's hand and turned to look at Margaret with pure astonishment.

"So, *you* are the Countess of Renwick? *You* are my sister?" he said with accusation in his voice.

Margaret inhaled sharply, holding her breath as she nodded and waited to see what he said next.

"Well, that explains why you did not want me to kiss you last night."

"Quite."

He moved towards her and placed his hands on both sides of her arms while asking, in a softer way this time, "Why did you not tell me in the beginning?"

"I made multiple attempts, but I was not even certain until last night at the window that you would be able to get your memories back. And you were tired and I thought it could wait," Margaret finished lamely.

The truth was that she was afraid. She could have said it at any point the previous night, but she had worried that, if he did not get his memories back, she would not be able to handle it. If he did not know who she was, it somehow made it easier to accept that possibility.

Pierre approached Randall and looked at him for several moments before saying, "I think it time I introduce myself. I am Pierre Girald, the Vidame of Demoulin."

Randall furrowed his brows together and asked, "Why does that name sound familiar?"

"Because Pierre was your best friend until you went missing. You were in boarding school together."

"Truly?" Randall asked.

Pierre nodded. "I am glad to see you, Randall. You may not remember me, but we were very close growing up. I hope that we can build a new friendship in the future."

"I think I would like that."

Jackie moved towards the door, pulling Pierre behind her. She said in parting, "I think we will leave you two alone. I will stop by later, Margaret." She turned and hastily left the room.

"It seems that you have known all along that, if what you say is true, we are joint heirs to the Renwick title. How is that?"

"Actually, we are not joint heirs. I inherited the title when our father died a year ago, but because you are my brother, I want to relinquish it to you. It should have been yours if the sea had not taken you from us. If we were in England, we could have the title legally changed back over to you, but since we are in France, it is impossible. However, having it legally changed is just a formality and no one will question it."

"What will you do without the title?"

"I am getting married soon, and Michel will take care of Henry and me. Most noblewomen must marry because they do not have a title of their own. This will be no different."

"I do not want you to have to marry someone just so he provides for you and my nephew. I am your brother, and I want to take care of my family."

She smiled, realizing that even without his memories,

Randall was still being the protective brother she had always depended upon. It was good to feel sheltered again.

"Tell me about our family, if you do not mind."

"I was born Lady Margaret Elaine Wellesley, twin to you, Lord Randall Thomas Wellesley. Our parents were Lord Stewart Patrick Wellesley, the Earl of Renwick, and Lady Charlotte Elaine Sunton, Baroness of Ramlin. Our mother died giving birth to us and our father died last year from consumption."

Walking over to her liquor cabinet, Randall poured himself a drink. She noticed that it was brandy. He always had been partial to brandy.

She remembered when they were nine and he was home from boarding school. They had sneaked into their father's study when he had been in town for a meeting, getting into his supply of spirits and trying every last one. They had been unbelievably drunk and Randall kept going back to the brandy.

Margaret had been sure when their father found them that he was going to give them a sound thrashing. But instead he laughed, patted them on the back, and told them they got a one-time pass to drink like that. He always did have a soft hand when it came to punishment.

"Why did you decide to drink the brandy? It is not your typical dock tavern drink."

"I do not know. I have had it on occasion, and I find it to be my favorite drink." He winked at her. "Although I would never admit that down at the docks."

She smiled. "We have both always been partial to brandy. We got caught once drinking all of Father's liquors." She stood up and walked over to the window. "I miss him."

He poured himself another and one for her as well, then walked over to the window and handed it to her.

"Is he buried back in England?"

Saddened, she nodded as a flood of grief washed over her as she thought about the loss of their father. "I did not have much time before I had to leave to come here. It has been hard not being able to go to his grave to visit."

"I am sorry."

Margaret flinched at her brother's unattached tone.

"You do not remember him, do you?"

He shook his head. "I am afraid not."

"You probably do not remember our home either."

"Again, no."

She turned to face him and asked in a voice that she could not quite keep the pleading from, "Do you remember anything from your childhood?"

He furrowed his brows in concentration as he thought. A few moments passed, and he replied, "I do recall one thing. I do not know why, but I seem to remember the scent of lavender. It was thick and it surrounded me, but not in a smothering way. Actually, when I got sick here in France, that scent would fill my dreams and I would feel safe and secure. It comforted me. Do you know why I would dream about that?"

Tears welled up in the corner of Margaret's violet eyes.

She nodded as they slowly cascaded down her cheeks. She attempted to brush them away but more followed in their place.

"Our mother wore lavender perfume. She loved the smell so much she had trees planted around the family estate. There were trees outside our windows, and when the wind blew, the scent from the blossoms would float into our rooms. When I was older, Father gave me mother's bottle of perfume, and I have worn it ever since."

Hesitantly at first, Randall leaned forward and sniffed her neck. Then he inhaled more deeply and leaned back in recognition.

"That is the scent. That is the exact smell I remember."

She saw sadness enter his eyes, and she realized he too felt the loss of not ever knowing their mother and losing the last years he could have had with their father.

A bit awkwardly at first, he dabbed at Margaret's tears as she gave him a lopsided half smile.

He winked at her, then asked, "What was that smile for?"

"For your kindness." She put her hand on the side of his cheek while looking into his eyes. "For years I did not cry because I considered it a bond between us. I never let myself cry because you were everything to me and I needed something to hold on to that was just for you. My tears for many years were only for you."

"I do not want you to ever have to cry again."

"I will not have to now that you are here."

"I hate that it has taken us this long to find each other."

"Yes, but now we have, and I want us to make the most of it. No dwelling in the past and what we have lost. We need to concentrate on the future."

"You are right." He leaned forward and sniffed her scent again. "But I cannot help wanting to know more about our family. What did she look like?"

"Who? Mother?"

"Yes."

"Like us. People have always told me that I look exactly like mother. And since you and I are almost identical, she looked like you as well."

"We look alike?"

She took him over to the mirror and pointed at their reflection.

His mouth dropped open as he stared at their images in disbelief. They were so similar, from their jet-black hair to their deep violet eyes. Side by side, they stood as matching figures that had been separated for far too long.

Margaret laughed. "We are not only brother and sister, but we are also twins. I am the female version of you." Thinking twice about her comment, she amended her statement. "Well, physically anyway."

It was his turn to laugh. "Can I help it if I love to make love?"

She raised her eyebrow in distaste for his comment. "Maybe I should let you get to know Jackie better. You are similar in at least that."

In admiration, he asked, "Really? A woman who likes to make love as much as me?"

"More, I daresay."

"I am impressed, and I assure you that is a rare task indeed." He pulled his sister by the arm over to the sofa. "So, tell me everything. I want to know about our family, your life, how you came to live in France, how you found me."

"We do have a lot of catching up to do. But first, there is something that I have wanted to do since I saw you last night." She reached over and pulled him into an embrace. "I have missed you so much."

He hugged her back, and after a few moments said in a confused but sincere voice, "I do not know *how*, but I feel that I have missed you as well."

"I think that it is time I tell you about yourself."

She was so overjoyed that God had chosen to give her back her brother. She thought she was going to spend the rest of her life with no family left, no one who had known her since she was born. But her brother was back, and she was going to do whatever it took to make sure their relationship was completely restored.

CHAPTER 18

While reading in the study, Margaret heard a soft knock at the door. She looked up. "Come in."

It was Pierre. She raised an eyebrow at him and asked, "What are you doing here?"

He picked up a ceramic knickknack from the entry table and idly shifted it back and forth between his hands. Margaret knew Pierre well and could tell he was contemplating how to phrase what he was going to say next.

"I came to say goodbye, actually." Apparently, saying it bluntly was how he planned to say farewell. Margaret could not believe it; after all this time of pursuing her, he was finally giving up. Even though it was what she thought she wanted, somehow it still hurt.

If she was honest with herself, she was not surprised. She was astonished that he had stuck it out as long as he had, considering how unbearable she had been making it for him. She knew it must have been painful for him to watch other men chase her and know that she might choose one of them to marry.

Because part of her still hoped she might have heard him wrong, she asked, "What do you mean 'goodbye'?"

"I am leaving for England tomorrow."

"Why?"

"I have some business matters to attend to there."

"How long will you be gone?"

He paused for a moment, then replied, "Indefinitely." She could hear the pain in his voice that he was trying to hide.

"Oh, I see." And she did. He hated seeing her with another man. He did not like watching the marquis spend time with the woman he wanted, the woman whom everyone suspected he loved.

"I can no longer stay here and watch you with the marquis. Before you were engaged to him, I thought I had a chance to convince you that we were meant to be together. But now I know it is hopeless. Before I go though, I wanted to tell you one thing. I feel I need to leave knowing that I told you exactly how I feel."

"All right, what is it?" she asked, even though she knew he was about to make a declaration that had been a long time coming.

"I love you, Margaret. You may not want to hear it, but it is true. I love you, and your refusal to allow yourself to love me in return is the real reason why I am leaving."

He turned around to leave, and she started to reach out to stop him but refrained. It was better this way. She did not want to give him any false hope.

Instead, she said softly as he opened the door, "I will miss you. I have come to count on you being there, and our friendship means a great deal to me."

Pierre stood still for a moment but kept his back to her. "It has to me as well, but I know I cannot be around you without wanting more."

He stepped through the door and shut it behind him without looking back. She stared at it for several seconds without moving.

He was gone. Just like that, Pierre was no longer in her life. It seemed as if those she held most dear disappeared without a moment's notice. It was as if something came along and wiped away their very existence before she could even take a breath.

Margaret blinked, trying to hold back the tears that threatened to fall. She walked over and sat down in one of the chairs in the entryway.

She was taking in what had just occurred when Jackie barged into the room, saying, "Margaret, you better be ready because...." Her voice trailed off as she saw the tears in Margaret's eyes. "What? What is the matter?"

"Pierre just came by to inform me that he is leaving for England."

With an unnerving upbeat tone, Jackie replied, "I know, he came by and told me this afternoon. Why are you crying, you ninny? He is just going over there to lick his wounds. He will be back shortly."

Margaret shook her head. "No, he told me that he was going to be there *indefinitely*. He left because of me, Jackie," Margaret said in a voice riddled with guilt. "I drove him away!"

"He is a grown man, and he needs to learn to deal with rejection. It is a fact of life that he has needed to face for a long time. He needed to learn sooner or later that he is not always going to get what he wants. Anyhow, he will not be able to stay away for long. I know my cousin, and his home has and will always be in France."

With a deep frown, Margaret looked down at her hands gripped in her lap. "I know, but I am going to miss him."

"Mon chéri, you are not in love with my cousin, are you?"

Margaret's eyes snapped up and grew wide with disbelief. "Of course not! It is just that I had not expected him to leave like this."

But part of her had to admit that, if she had let herself, she could have indeed fallen in love with Pierre. He was able to get under her skin in a way that frightened her—partly because it reminded her of how she had felt about the duke so long ago. She had desired him the same way she wanted Pierre, and when Witherton had done the unthinkable and violated her the way he had, a piece of her had been destroyed. She did not trust the way she used to before he ruined her.

Jackie grabbed her friend's arm and pulled her up. "You

are just going to have to shrug this off. Pierre will get over all of this, and you will be getting married soon, so do not dwell on his departure. Nothing is ever perfect."

Margaret had been spending a significant amount of time working with Randall on informing him about his past. Michel understood her need to focus on Randall for the time being, rather than preparations for their wedding. She wanted her brother to be fully himself before she moved forward with any other plans. She was disappointed his memories were not returning as she had anticipated, but remained hopeful they could in the future.

"Randall, are you in here?"

"Yes, I will be right out, Margaret."

She waited in the sitting room of her brother's bedroom chambers. It had been a week, and although she and Randall were growing close, she knew that they both wished his memories would return. Without them, it felt as if there was a missing piece to their lives and nothing would be complete without them.

Randall emerged from his bedroom and asked, "What are you doing here, my sister?"

"I was wondering if you would like to go on a ride with me today. I thought we could take a carriage over to the stables and then ride a set of Michel's horses. It has been far longer than I like between visits."

"Did we ride often when we lived in England?"

She smiled, saying, "Yes, living in the country, it was a constant pastime."

"Then I should probably be good at it?"

"You were excellent. Perhaps not as good as me, but no one was in our province."

"My, my, are we not boastful?" Randall laughed as he jokingly patted his sister on the back.

"No, I am not 'boastful,' as you put it. I am self-assured when it comes to horses. They are my area of expertise."

"I will have to take your word on that since I cannot remember."

The jest fell flat on Margaret, as she did not like when he joked about his memory loss.

As they rode in the carriage to the stables, Margaret looked out the window of the carriage at the city. It was so full with people constantly coming and going from all the shops and cafés. She was not sure if she would ever get used to all the busyness.

Margaret began to get excited in anticipation as they pulled into the carriage house at the stables. She missed riding, but it was much harder to find time to ride between all her social commitments and spending time with Henry. She planned to bring him to the stables once he was a bit older, but she knew it was not safe yet.

The twins made their way to the stable office. They knew who she was, and she was sure they had already sent a stable-hand to start the process for them to ride.

An older man with brown hair peppered with grey was at the front desk. He smiled at her. "Good afternoon, Lady Margaret. I see you have a guest with you this afternoon who is not Lord Robineau."

Realizing it might seem inappropriate, she quickly said, "This is my brother, Lord Randall Wellesley, the Earl of Renwick."

"Pleased to make your acquaintance, my lord." The older man looked down at something at his desk, then added, "There is an additional matter I need to discuss with you, my lady."

"Yes, of course. What is it?"

"It seems we have a shipment here for you."

"A shipment? What do you mean?" she asked, flummoxed.

"It seems you have a gift waiting for you. It is located in stall number seven."

"May I inquire as to what it is?"

"I am sorry, my lady, but there are specific instructions that say you must go there in person. I am to hand you this note that you are to open only after you have seen the gift."

It must have been an engagement gift from Michel. He knew she loved horses and must have bought her one. What a wonderful man she was marrying.

They arrived at the stall and Margaret meekly opened the door to the stall. She knew better than to go charging into the stall of a horse she did not know.

From out of the shadows appeared the most unexpected surprise. It was Charlie. *How could this be?*

Charlie moved towards Margaret and nuzzled directly into the hollow of her neck. Margaret wrapped her arms around her most prized mare and started to softly cry.

Randall reached out his hand and supportively placed it on Margaret's shoulder. "Are you all right? What is going on, Margaret?"

"I just cannot believe it."

"Believe what?"

"This is my horse, Charlotte's Pride. I had to leave her behind in England. I thought I would never see her again."

"How did she get here?"

"I have no idea," Margaret replied. Then, remembering the letter she had been handed, she pulled it free from her pant pocket.

Margaret gingerly opened the envelope and pulled out the contents.

My dearest Margaret,

I hope this letter finds you well. During my time here in England, I was able to locate Charlie for you. I know how much you miss her, and when I found it possible, I could not resist getting her for you. I hope she brings you much joy and would like you to consider this my engagement gift.

With my undying love,

Pierre

She could not believe it. After several weeks of being away, Pierre was still thinking of her. She had always thought he was only infatuated with her, but this made her wonder if he really did love her. It did not change her mind, as she knew the marquis was her best chance for obtaining a Christian husband who provided security, but it did make her realize that Pierre was a kind man. She truly hoped he would find happiness without her.

"Margaret, who did this for you?"

"Charlie was procured and given to me by Pierre."

Randall nodded. "That was kind of him. I wished he had stayed in France longer so I could have gotten to know him again."

Feeling responsible for Pierre's departure, she said, "It is my fault he left in the way he did. He wanted to court me, and I was not receptive to it."

"Why not? Nothing against Michel, but would you be happier with Pierre?"

"I care for Pierre greatly but cannot see a future with him. We have different beliefs, and Michel can provide security and protection far above what Pierre can offer."

"But is compatibility not more important than feeling safe?"

"Not for me. I would give up everything to keep my family safe."

"What do you mean by that comment? Has something in the past caused you to feel unsafe, Margaret?"

To avoid talking about Catherine or the duke, she replied, "When Father died and I found out the family estate was impoverished, I felt that way."

"I am sorry you ever felt unsafe. I will make it my goal to never let it happen again."

"You have always protected me, ever since we were little. Some things never change."

"When Pierre was here, he mentioned we were close growing up."

"Yes, he was one of our playmates when we were children, whenever his family visited England. His father and ours started out as business partners and became friends through their projects together."

"I hate this, Margaret. I feel like my memories are always just out of grasp. I want to remember so badly, but I feel like I am never able to make it happen."

"Give it time, Randall. It will come with time."

Rubbing his hand down Charlie's mane, he said, "I have to say, Pierre seemed like a nice fellow when I re-met him. But even for a good family friend, this seems to be an elaborate gift. If you do not mind me asking, are you sure there is not more than friendship there?"

Margaret looked at her brother with astonishment. He

always had an exceptional way of ascertaining what was really going on in a situation just under the surface.

"He thinks he is in love with me."

"Are *you* in love with *him*?"

Margaret adamantly shook her head in denial. "No, I did not let myself. I need someone who sees eye to eye on important aspects of life. I need a man who believes in God the way I do. It was difficult to have him leave under such painful circumstances, but it was for the best."

"You had not mentioned that you were religious."

Margaret could hear the disapproving tone in Randall's voice. She did not like being called "religious," as it made her think of people constantly forcing their views on everyone around them. Instead, she considered herself a follower of Christ. She believed and would share her views if someone asked, but she never wanted to upset people. She truly believed that, through the way she lived her life, people would see Jesus in her.

She had made the mistake of hiding her spiritual side from Pierre and Jackie. She refused to do it again.

"Yes, Rand," she admitted, using the nickname she had for him since they were children, "I have recently become a devoted Christian. I try to go to church regularly, and my relationship with God is of the upmost importance to me. I struggle sometimes with living my life according to the Bible, but after accepting the Lord's offer of salvation, the emptiness I used to feel inside has gone away. It was our father's dying wish that I find my own way to God. He left me a letter begging me to accept Jesus as my lord and savior. I could let you read it sometime if you would like."

"Margaret, I appreciate your sentiment, but organized religion and I have never gotten along. It is not to say I do not believe in God, only that I do not feel the need to go to church to prove it."

She could see that Randall was not receptive to what she was saying, so she opted to change the subject. "I think it is time for us to go riding."

Brother and sister rode into the fields near the stables, and she was transported back to a time when they were children. It was picturesque, as the wildflowers were in bloom and lay in bunches sprinkled throughout the green meadows.

They laughed as they took turns taking the lead and hopped over puddles and fallen logs. It was nice to have a riding partner again as Michel did not enjoy the equestrian life, being from the city. He kept the majority of his horses as investments and to pull his carriages.

After running full steam, it was time to slow the horses and let them take a break.

Margaret watched her brother, who looked entirely at home atop the stallion he was riding. It was nice to be doing something so relaxing with him. They had spent hours in her home trying to force memories that may never come. She had to accept that just having him back, even without them, was enough.

God, please help me accept my brother as he is and not be

saddened by what I cannot change. I find my hope through you, so I ask that you give me peace with how things are right now. You do tell us that we have not because we ask not, so I am asking you, Lord. If it be your will, please bring my brother back to me fully.

"Thank you for suggesting this, Mags. I really needed it."

Pulling her horse to a stop, Margaret stared at Randall. "Why did you just call me that?"

"Call you what?"

"Mags?"

"I did not realize I had." He thought about it for a moment, then continued, "I used to call you that when we were little, did I not?"

Margaret put her gloved hand to her chest and asked, "Do you *remember* calling me that?"

Several seconds passed as Randall concentrated, "Yes, I do remember. I recall going riding with you. Going riding today must be what caused this memory to come back."

"I cannot believe it. I was just starting to accept that you might never regain your memories and now this happened."

She realized that it was not luck or anything she did but God answering her prayers. It was His will for Randall to remember his past. She was grateful beyond words.

CHAPTER 19

*M*argaret was anxious to see how her brother looked in his formal attire. The dinner for his reintroduction back into aristocratic society was either going to help him gain favor in the right social circles or cause him to not be entirely recognized. She hoped it would be the former and that he would make a splendid splash.

She thought about the last week. Bit by bit, Randall's memories were coming back to him. He already remembered a great deal, but there were patches in his memory that he had not regained. She was sure they would come in time.

It had been relatively easy to convince everyone that he was her brother. Once he was dressed in the proper clothes with the right haircut, it was obvious that he was her twin.

Jackie had stopped spending time with other men, including Monte, and focused her attention on Randall. She was smitten with him, and he seemed to be intrigued by her.

It was going to be interesting to see what came of that situation.

"Can I come in, Randall?"

"Yes, I am still finishing getting ready." Margaret entered her brother's dressing room as he said, "You know, it still takes getting used to being called that."

He finished adjusting his vest in the mirror, and then turned around to face Margaret. He lifted his glass of brandy to his lips and took a swig.

She smirked. "Really, well, I cannot even imagine calling you 'Pepe.' Why ever did you pick that ridiculous name?"

Randall shrugged. "I have no idea. I got tired of not having a name, and everyone calling me 'boy' all the time, so one night when I was drunk—"

She interrupted him. "You were getting drunk even back then?"

"Once a lush, always a lush, my dear. Anyway, as I was saying, I was dancing with a whor—woman and she asked me my name. So, I told her I did not have one and asked her what she would like to call me. She said she was always partial to the name 'Pepe,' and there you have it."

She shook her head. "One day a woman is going to be your downfall."

Just at that moment, Jackie knocked at the door, asking, "May I enter?"

Randall and Margaret both burst out in laughter as Randall stammered, "Come in."

Jackie entered the room with a frown on her face. In irritated confusion, she asked, "What are you laughing about?"

He looked from Jackie to his sister and said pointedly, "Perhaps you are right."

Margaret replied to Jackie, "Nothing."

Randall walked over to Jackie and took her hand. He kissed the top of it and said, "You look incredibly lovely tonight, Jacquelyn." He insisted on calling her by her full first name, and surprisingly, she liked it.

Jackie blushed like a young schoolgirl, and Margaret raised an eyebrow in amazement. She had never seen her friend blush before. Jackie must be really taken with her brother to react that way.

"Thank you, Randy," Jackie replied. Margaret waited for her brother to correct her, but he did not. He had always hated it when people shortened his name, and he still did. Albert had called him Randy, as the servant had when he was a little boy, and Randall told him not to do it again.

Up until now, Margaret had been the only one who had been able to call him anything but Randall, her affectionate nickname for him being Rand and his Maggie or Mags for her.

She was just the tiniest bit jealous and so, trying to divert his attention, she said, "Rand, I think we should make our way outside to the carriage."

Randall looked at Jackie and asked, "Will you stay after the dinner a bit so that I may talk with you?"

She nodded. "I will wait for you both in the carriage."

"I appreciate it." He let go of her hand and watched as Jacquelyn left the room. He then turned to face his sister. "All right, Maggie, you have my undivided attention now."

She blushed at how easy he perceived her ploy. He knew her so well, even after only a week of having his memories back. But then, they were twins after all.

"That was not my intent—"

"Save it, Mags, I know you and how possessive you are over me. You always have been. Even when we were children you were like that. I remember when the little servant girls followed me around, you would stomp your foot with your hands on your hips and demand that they leave me alone."

She blushed even deeper. "They were interrupting our game, Rand, and I wanted to finish. You know how I hate to not finish games."

He snickered. "Or lose. As I recall, you were losing at the time."

Margaret shrugged off his comment. "Your memory must still be faulty. I never lose, especially to you."

He rolled his eyes and laughed. "Let us be on our way."

"I agree."

They were having dinner at Maison D'orée on the Boulevard des Italiens. It was one of the most exclusive restaurants in all of Paris, and Margaret had one of their largest private dining rooms reserved for the evening.

The restaurant had lush white walls with large mirrors and golden furnishings and statues. In their private room, there were tasteful sofas as well as a magnificently large table set with exquisite gilded plates and crystal goblets.

With Margaret on one arm and Jackie on the other, the threesome made their way to their seats at the table. As they sat down, Michel joined them and sat next to Margaret. It was going to be a night to remember, and Margaret was glad to finally be reunited with her brother and share it openly.

Once all of the prestigious guests had arrived and were seated in their assigned places, Margaret stood up to address everyone. "It is my distinct pleasure to introduce all of you to my twin brother, Lord Randall Wellesley, the Earl of Renwick. As many of you know, he was presumed dead over eight years ago, and due to his loss of memory we were unable to reconnect until just recently. I hope all of you find a place in your hearts for him, as he has always had a place in mine."

There were several murmurs and "ahhhs" that were heard throughout the room.

Margaret held up her glass of wine and said, "A toast to Lord Wellesley, Earl of Renwick."

Everyone raised their glasses, and clinks and cheers resounded throughout the place.

Margaret sat back down and nodded to the servers. All of their plates were placed in front of them at the same time. As the guests began to nibble on the first course of the meal, Randall leaned over and whispered to his sister, "Thank you so much for everything, Maggie."

"Of course, Rand. You deserve it."

Jackie started talking to Randall and Margaret could see that the two of them were growing closer.

Michel smiled at Margaret and said, "I am glad that your brother is being received so well."

"I appreciate that, Michel. It means a great deal that you are behind us in this."

"You know that I want you to be happy. You are a wonderful woman, Margaret, and you are going to make an exceptional wife. You already make an outstanding mother, and I cannot wait to have more children with you." She waited for him to say he loved her. She had been waiting for him to say he loved her since he proposed, but the words never crossed his lips.

Although, considering she was not in love with him, it was quite a double standard to expect him to feel something for her that would be most undeniably one-sided. She convinced herself that she could and would grow to love him romantically in time, despite the fact that she did not feel the spark she had with either Richard in the beginning, Henry in the end, or Pierre while she was in France.

Part of her believed that she was closed off to the idea of falling in love because of what happened to her in the past. If he could tell her that he loved her, maybe it could break through her defenses and help her be able to love again. She waited for the words, but he did not say them. Instead, he slightly squeezed her hand and turned back to his meal.

It was all right, as she had time to find out if he loved her. They were not getting married until two months' time.

She knew that if he still had not said it by their wedding day, it was also possible that he could grow to love her in time. At least, many couples that had arranged marriages grew to love one another. They could do the same, could they not?

After the dinner, several guests, including Margaret and Michel, made their way over to the large sofas and sat down to converse.

"Your brother looks really content. I have heard that he has gained a whole flock of admiring women tonight."

"Yes, I have heard the same thing. Unfortunately for them, he is soon to be spoken for, I think."

Just as she said that, Jackie walked up to the group of women surrounding Randall. She gave each of them a warning look and put her arm through his as he bowed and made his excuses. The soon-to-be-official couple made their way over to a private corner of the room. Margaret noticed them laughing, probably over her intercession.

"I see what you mean."

"I hope this does not complicate anything between us, Michel."

"Why would it?"

"Jackie has stopped spending time with other men, including your brother. I hope you will not hold it against me since it is my brother who has gained her attention."

"You have no control over either of them, just as I have no control over my brother."

"I am glad you are able to look at it that way. I have to

admit, I think Randall and Jacquelyn are perfect for each other."

"Perhaps, or perhaps they will end up killing each other considering how much they drink and fight."

"That just means they enjoy life and are passionate for each other."

"You are overly romantic, Margaret. That type of passion does one of two things: dwindles out or burns you up. Neither option seems very appealing to me."

Margaret averted her eyes so that he was unable to see the sadness in them. By his statement, she realized that it was not that Michel could not love her, but that he refused to allow himself to do so. She finally had to acknowledge that no matter how hard she tried to make him love her, it was never going to happen.

CHAPTER 20

*C*amille Saint-Saens, a famous composer and pianist, was performing for the French elite. He had been a child prodigy and was considered one of France's premier musicians. Margaret was eager to watch him play as he had a growing reputation of being tantalizing in the way his hands glided across the keys of the piano.

Margaret listened to Jackie recite all the musician's achievements to Randall, who was already boozy from several glasses of brandy, as they rode in their carriage. The concert was being held on the Avenue Montaigne in a large garden. When they arrived, the area was lit by hundreds of gas lamps and the stage was set and ready for the concert.

Michel was waiting for them as their carriage arrived outside the garden. He reached up and helped Margaret out.

"Good evening, Margaret. You look beautiful."

Margaret was wearing a dark green corseted satin gown

with velvet tassels and piping along the edges. Half her hair was pinned up while the rest was loose, tumbling down her back in curls.

"Thank you, Michel."

As they walked to their seats, he leaned towards Margaret and whispered discreetly, "I need to forewarn you. My brother is here tonight, and I anticipate he will not be happy to see your brother with Jackie. I told him not to make a scene, but he is rather impulsive, as you well know."

"Do you think he will say something?"

"Most likely, but honestly, I am more apprehensive concerning what he might do."

Worried, Margaret said, "I need to caution my brother." But before she could turn around to do so, she saw Monte approaching their group.

"I see you brought your new paramour with you, Jackie."

Michel glared at his brother and scolded him. "Monte, I realize that you are upset, but do not be disrespectful towards Margaret's brother."

Ignoring Michel's rebuke, he continued to aggress Jackie and Randall. "You really should think twice about coming to these events together. These are my friends, and this is my world."

Jackie looked at Monte with exasperation. "Monte, the time we spent together was never permanent. Why are you reacting this way?"

"I will not let you throw me off to allow you to carry on with this English knave. You may want him to think what we had was not genuine, but we both know I was preparing to propose to you."

Jackie gasped as her eyes grew wide with shock. She glanced over at Randall and then back to Monte. Shaking her head in rebuff, she countered, "That is not true. I was unaware of your plans. I am sorry that you have been hurt by my calling off our arrangement, but my heart lies elsewhere now."

As Jackie started to turn to leave, Monte grabbed her by the arm. "Your heart used to lie with me, as did your body. If you are trying to convince everyone else differently, I will not let you get away with it."

Randall grabbed Monte's hand forcefully and removed it from Jackie's arm. "You should not lay hands on a lady like that."

Monte snorted. "You are mistaken. She is no lady."

Without warning, Randall reached back and swung a closed fist at Monte's face. The force sent Monte flying backwards and he hit the ground with a hard thud.

"Where I come from, gentlemen do not speak about women that way, either."

Randall gently placed his hand under Jackie's elbow and started to guide her towards their seats, but before they reached them, Monte regained his footing and lunged towards Randall's back. The men fell to the floor in a heap, and Monte pulled Randall over as he swung at him. Randall raised his arms defensively and blocked Monte's first blow. Quickly, Randall returned him blow for blow.

Jackie started screaming, "Stop, you two. This is ridiculous. You are making a scene." But neither man was listening as they continued hitting each other.

Margaret watched in disbelief as the fight went on until Michel grabbed Monte and tried to pull him off Randall unsuccessfully. Two additional gentlemen from the growing crowd around them helped Michel break up the brawl.

Both men had scrapes, bruises, and welts on their faces. Margaret ran over to her brother and asked, "Are you okay, Rand?"

He nodded. "This is not the first fight I have gotten into, and it probably will not be the last."

"I am going to make my excuses to Michel and take you home."

"Do not do that, Mags. I know how much you wanted to come to this concert. I can manage to get home by myself."

Jackie leaned in and said, "I will go with him and take care of him. It is the least I can do to thank him for defending my honor."

Hesitantly, Margaret consented. Monte was cursing under his breath while one of his cronies took him under the arm and led him away. Margaret heard him mention going to a gambling club as he was in no mood to listen to music.

Michel and Margaret sat down just as the musicians began to tune their instruments. Michel leaned over and said, "I cannot believe our brothers just got into a fight over the same woman."

Margaret shook her head. "Jackie tends to have that effect on men."

"Have I ever told you that I am grateful that you are not like that?"

"Yes, you have made it quite clear that you are not interested in passionate displays of any nature."

"I am glad we see eye to eye on that."

Margaret refrained from correcting Michel. She did not want men fighting over her, but she was not opposed to a man caring enough to defend her. Her late husband had failed in that regard and did not give her the benefit of the doubt. Michel said he was trying to learn to fight for her, but she worried he would fail in the same way. She envied Jackie for having found that type of love with her brother and wondered if she could live without it.

Motty came to talk to Margaret while she was playing with Henry in the garden. "My lady, as you know, I have been taking Henry to the park most afternoons, allowing Sarah time to do any chores she needs to do. While there a few days ago, a noblewoman approached me and asked if I was interested in taking a position as a governess in her household. I told her I would have to talk to you, and she said she would want a letter of recommendation from you to prove my competency for the employment."

"Do you want to take the position?"

"You have always taken good care of me, my lady, and I care for all of you so much."

"Thank you, but that does not answer the question." Margaret waited for Motty's response, which did not come. "Please, be honest with me. You will not hurt my feelings."

"The placement pays considerably more than what I currently make, and it would place me in one of the highest positions in their household."

"Then I think you must take it. You deserve this, Motty. You have always been a diligent and loyal servant, and when you chose to come with me to France, it touched me beyond words. If this is what you want, you have my approval."

"Thank you, my lady. I will never forget your kindness over the past several years."

"This is not goodbye. You can visit us any time you wish. You are our family, Motty. That will never change, even with you taking opportunities presented to you."

Margaret leaned over and hugged the young woman she had grown to consider like a sister. She would miss her, but she knew it was best for Motty to let her take this monumental step, even if it meant leaving them behind.

CHAPTER 21

When Margaret went looking for her brother, she guessed correctly she would find him reading in the library.

He had been spending a great deal of time reading after moving in with Margaret, citing that he had eight years of lack of knowledge that he needed to remedy.

"Rand, I was wondering. It is such a beautiful day, would you care to go on a picnic with Henry and me?"

"Jacquelyn is coming over for tea, but I bet I could persuade her to go with us to the park instead."

"That would be lovely. Henry will love going with Uncle Randall and Aunt Ja-Ja."

"She is not Aunt Ja-Ja yet."

Margaret winked at Randall and said sarcastically, "I am sure that will not be for long."

"Are you fishing for something, my dear sister?"

She did not want to divulge the fact that Jackie had asked her to find out if and when Randall would be partial to proposing to her. She had to concede that she was curious as well.

"I only notice that you have been spending a great deal of time with my dear friend Jackie. Since that is the case, I wondered when it might be progressing to more."

Randall chucked under his breath. "You can tell Jacquelyn that I will not be duped that easily into giving up the details of any plans I may or may not be preparing in regards to our relationship status."

"What plans might those be?" Jackie asked as she stood at the door to the library.

"Ah, there you are, my sweet. We were just talking about you."

"I heard as much, which is why I asked what plans you were discussing with Margaret."

"We have a change of plans today. We are going to have a picnic in the park with Maggie and Henry."

Jacquelyn pouted with her hands on her hips. "Somehow, I do not think that was the plan you were discussing."

He smirked at Jackie. "I bet you would like to know, but I am sorry to disappoint you. I do have to keep some secrets to myself."

Jackie rolled her eyes and said, "It does not seem that I will be getting any answers from him right now, so now is as good as time as any to go have a picnic."

After arriving at the park, Margaret sat on a blanket,

watching her son ride on her brother's back, giggling as he pretended to neigh like a horse. It was wonderful being with them. She finally felt like she might have a happy future, worth all that she had been through. She was blessed with her son, brother, best friend, and soon a husband to complete their family.

"May I speak with you, Margaret?"

She looked up to see Michel standing near her. She did not expect him to be joining them.

"What are you doing here?"

"I had something I needed to discuss with you, so I went by your residence and your butler told me that you had come to the park."

Something in Michel's tone made her worry. He sounded distant and a little bit cold.

"Is something the matter, Michel?"

"May we go for a walk? I would rather discuss this matter in private."

"Of course."

He reached out his hand to her and helped her stand from the blanket. He let go of her as soon as she was on her feet. Margaret rested her hand on his arm and felt him stiffen under her touch. What was wrong?

"Some information regarding your past has been brought to my attention."

Margaret braced herself for what Michel was going to say. Her worst fears were coming true. Before she panicked, she needed to know how much he knew. Maybe it was not as bad as she thought.

"What are you referring to, Michel?"

"I am referring to why you came to France."

"You know why. My husband passed away and I came to look for my brother."

"It was not because you had been involved in a scandal back in England that had been suppressed to protect your late husband's family name?"

Margaret's heartbeat quickened and she started to feel faint. Perhaps it was time to panic. He seemed to know far more than she had anticipated.

"My husband had an enemy who chose to use me to destroy him."

"Is that why there are questions surrounding the paternity of your son?"

Sucking in a deep breath, Margaret held it. It stung to have someone question it out loud again. She thought she had left all of that behind her when she fled England, but she realized her past was never going to let her be happy.

"He is my late husband's child. There is no question as to that. Regarding what happened with my husband and the other man—"

"You mean the Duke of Witherton."

Perplexed by how much detail he knew about her past, she asked, "How do you know so much about my history?"

"Someone who thought I had a right to know before I married you told me."

The only person who knew the details around what happened to her was Pierre. How could he do this to her? He had said he loved her, and now he had hurt her in the most profound way by telling her deepest, darkest secret to the man she was going to marry. But that was just it, she realized; the whole purpose of him telling Michel about her past was to give him no choice but to leave her.

"I know it was Pierre who told you about my past, and although he is not lying, he has selfish reasons for telling you."

"I agree. That is why I confirmed the specifics since I knew his motives were not pure. But he was not mistaken, which means you have been withholding relevant information from me."

"I wanted to tell you, Michel, but I was scared."

"I can understand you not telling me in the beginning. It is not something you disclose until you are sure you can trust the person. But after I shared with you what happened with my sister, I thought we could trust one another. I gave you ample opportunities to tell me the whole truth, but you chose to remain quiet. It feels as if trust only goes one way between us."

Tears began to form in the corners of Margaret's eyes. She hated that she had hurt Michel, and now because she had made the mistake of not confiding in him, he no longer trusted her.

"I am so sorry. It is not only because I was afraid. I was also worried that you would see me differently after you knew. The way you looked at me, you saw me in such a pure manner. I did not want you to see me as tainted."

Another noble couple passed by them on the garden path and nodded in their direction. Margaret and Michel nodded in return, and Michel waited until they were no longer within range of hearing before continuing. "Margaret, I am a forgiving man. I have a great capacity to overlook many faults."

It sounded good on the surface, but the truth was, Margaret did not want a man to accept her in spite of her past, but love her because she had survived it. She knew she was a stronger person because of it, and she wanted to be married to someone that loved that about her.

"That is just it, Michel. I do not feel I need forgiveness. I never did anything wrong. I was a casualty of what the duke did *to* us. He is a horrible, evil man, and I can hardly stand to talk about him, but I want you to know what happened. He *forced* himself on me, and he lied to trick my husband into thinking I did it willingly. It was one of the worst moments in my life, only superseded when the duke killed my husband. I only found out I was pregnant after my husband was gone. To make matters worse, Catherine, my husband's sister, threatened to take my son if he was the Rolantry heir, and if not, to tell the duke so he could take him from me instead."

"Is that why you left England after your son was born, to escape before either of them could take him from you?"

Margaret nodded. "Do you want to end our engagement?"

She did not know what she would do if he said yes, but she refused to beg him to stay with her. She may end up penniless and alone, but she still would have her dignity.

"I have to confess, when I came to speak to you about this, I believed I was going to end our engagement. But after hearing what you went through and why, I believe you are innocent of any wrongdoing."

He stopped and looked at her for several seconds. "I want to believe in you, Margaret. I have come to care a great deal for you."

"And I, you, Michel. I am grateful that you were willing to listen to me, and I promise not to keep anything from you in the future."

"I appreciate that. Honesty is paramount to a lasting marriage."

"In that case, I do need to tell you something else."

"What is it?"

"The duke has been dispatching mercenaries to track us down. The night I found my brother, they took me hostage and planned to give me over to Witherton. Randall was able to free me before that happened and the men were... taken care of permanently."

"Do you need me to intervene?"

"No, I had an investigator handle the situation."

"What is his name?"

"Josef Mulchere."

"I have heard of him. He is an excellent investigator. Do you need me to engage my contacts in this matter?"

"He told me he has it under control, and I believe him."

"I promise you, Margaret, if anyone comes after you, I will end them."

She believed Michel, and for the first time in a long time, she felt that she might truly be safe.

CHAPTER 22

Standing beside the Marquis de Badour, Margaret placed her hand in the bend of his arm, as she quietly waited for the announcement of their arrival at their engagement ball.

Something had shifted between them the day she told him about her past. She was fairly certain that it was due to the dissolution of her hope that he would ever love her. He promised to protect her, but he made no mention of love. She felt broken and trapped. She could not end the engagement because she needed the protection and safety his title and wealth provided. Not to mention that, if she did end their relationship, her reputation would be tarnished forever, and she would never be able to obtain a suitable match with or without love in the equation.

No, there was no way around it. She would have to make peace with the fact that she was going to live the rest of her life without being in love again. The marquis was a good man, kind and fair. And she had the consolation that she was loved at least once in her life by her first husband. She could survive this. She had survived worse.

The doors to the marquis's ballroom opened as his butler declared, "With great honor, presenting Lady Margaret Wellesley, sister to the Earl of Renwick, escorted by her fiancé, Lord Michel Robineau, the Marquis de Badour."

As they walked through the doors, they were surrounded by lights, smiles, and applause. Encircled by all their friends and family, Margaret had never felt so alone. She could not help but wonder if this was how she was going to feel for the rest of her life: standing in the middle of a filled room but feeling completely by herself.

Margaret followed Michel onto the dance floor to start the night off with the first dance. Everything felt like a duty, a chore. Nothing held pleasure for her anymore. She pasted on a smile and said all the right things, but deep inside she felt empty.

What would her father think of her right now? He had raised her better than this. The one thing he wanted most for her in life was to feel true love. Then, almost as a wave, the most important words she ever heard came flooding back into her mind. *"I want you to recognize that love is not self-serving or conceited. It does not remember our iniquities or think evil thoughts of others. Love is gracious and honest. It can withstand anything and always bears hope."*

Why had she not thought of that before? Her father had

shared his thoughts about what the Bible viewed love as, and there was no mention of physical attraction in the attributes of true love. The marquis did all of the actions of love. If she really considered how Michel treated her, it was obvious that he did love her, even if he did not realize it himself. She could build on that, especially with God's help.

Lord, help me to love my future husband and to accept him as he is, rather than constantly wanting something more. You have shown me he acts out love, which is so much more important than saying it. Help me to be content in that knowledge.

"Margaret, are you paying attention to the steps? I know this dance is new to you, but you usually pick them up so fast."

She looked at Michel for the first time in several minutes. "I was thinking how grateful I am to have you in my life."

He smiled down at her. "As I am to have you in mine."

Margaret observed Mulchere standing behind a group of gossipers. Recognizing the urgent look in his eyes, unnoticeable to Michel, she nodded to let Mulchere know she would be there in a moment.

As soon as the song finished, Margaret said, "Michel, in light of our conversation the other day at the park, I need you to escort me outside to the garden right now."

Michel looked at her quizzically but did not argue. He placed his hand under her elbow and guided her out into an excluded area of the garden.

"What is going on, Margaret?"

"Monsieur Mulchere is here, which means something is amiss."

Mulchere appeared from around the corner and approached the couple. He looked at Michel cautiously and waited for his cues from Margaret. "This is my fiancé, the Marquis de Badour. You may speak freely in front of him."

"Yes, certainly, my lady. I thought that our plan had worked. The men who had been searching for you have been gone for the past several weeks. But this morning, I was working on another case when I overheard another man asking about you. He was carrying a newspaper, one that had your picture on it from the night of your engagement party."

This was getting worse. How stupid could she have been to have two major parties with all of French society present when she was being hunted down? She did not want to even think about Witherton finding her, or possibly Catherine. If either one of them found her, they would not hesitate to ruin her life here in France and try to take Henry from her.

"Has anyone told them where I am?"

"I believe it is unwise for you to stay here in France. I think it would be best to leave the country for a while."

Her instincts told her to flee, but her mind knew better. She needed to stay here in order to marry Michel. His name would be the only thing that could protect her against her enemies. If she did not marry him, they would have nothing.

"I cannot leave. I am to be married in two months' time."

"But, my lady, if you do not, then they will find you."

Michel stepped forward. "Monsieur Mulchere, I am

aware of the situation, and I also have agents who can work in conjunction with your own to make sure no one finds Lady Margaret."

Margaret knew they needed to change their plans going forward. "We can move the wedding date closer, then take Henry and go on an extended trip to celebrate our marriage." She looked at Michel to see if he agreed with her plans. He nodded in agreement.

"From here on out, I would like you to keep me informed of the situation."

"As you wish, my lord."

"Thank you for informing me, Monsieur Mulchere. I appreciate all that you have done for me."

"Very well, my lady. I will be on my way." He started to leave but turned back around. "Do be careful, Lady Margaret, I fear that danger is just around the corner."

CHAPTER 23

*A*lthough she was grateful Michel agreed to move up their wedding, she had drained herself getting everything ready in a week's time.

"I am exhausted, Rand. I am so grateful that all of the big events are almost over. You are now a part of the nobility here in France, my engagement party was a smash, and I will be married by the end of the week."

Margaret was doing all of the planning for the wedding, and surprising even herself, managing to accomplish everything in quick order.

"Maggie, I am happy for you. But I hope you have the strength for one more event perhaps? I was thinking I might be married soon as well."

She jumped at his intriguing statement. "Are you going to ask Jackie to marry you?"

Randall sat down on the divan by the window in the

parlor, pulling Margaret beside him. He looked at her and beamed. "I think I am in love, Mags. I mean really in love. I have never felt this way about a woman." He grabbed Margaret's hands in excitement, continuing, "Yes, I am going to propose to her. Tomorrow night, as a matter of fact."

Margaret pressed her lips together, trying to hold back her emotions. She wanted to be happy for them, but part of her envied what they had so much. She knew she would never be able to find that again, especially with Michel.

"Congratulations, Rand, I am truly happy for you." She forced a smile and patted his hands that now lay in her lap.

"Maggie, what is the matter? I can see that something is bothering you."

"Nothing," she said defensively. "At least nothing that I am going to discuss with you."

He pulled his hands away, crossed his arms over his chest, and frowned in mock hurt.

"I am offended, dear sister, that you do not think that you can confide in me."

"It is nothing. I am just having a hard time, and I am dealing with a lot of things right now."

"Like what?"

She stood up from the desk and moved over to the window, looking out. She had been avoiding telling him about the whole Witherton, Henry, and Catherine situation. She hated talking about it, and she just wished the whole situation would go away. Besides, there was a good chance that Michel could take care of everything and she would not need to tell Randall the details of her past.

"Now I know something is wrong. You forget, we are twins and I do many of the same things. I always look out a window when something is bothering me. It is like looking for the answer out there when you cannot find one in here," he said as he patted his chest. "What is it? Tell me."

She turned around and said again, "Nothing, I am just nervous about the wedding, that is all."

"Maggie, I know you, and I can see something else is wrong."

Avoiding the subject, Margaret smiled and said, "Nothing is the matter. I want to discuss the details of this proposal. How are you going to do it?"

"Nice try, Mags, but you are not getting any information out of me. I want to surprise Jackie, and I know if I tell you, it is going to go directly back to her."

"Fine, I suppose I will hear all about it soon enough. I do have to ask, where did you acquire the money for a ring?"

"I won a tiny bit the night you found me. I used it to get this." He pulled a box out of his pocket, which contained a simple gold band.

Margaret knew Jackie would be content with whatever Randall gave her, but she also knew a countess would be expected to have a much more extravagant ring.

"Give me a moment, Rand. I will be right back." Margaret made her way to her chambers and went inside to her vanity. She unlocked a bottom drawer where she kept her jewelry and pulled out a ring box, then headed back to the study and sat down next to Randall.

"I have something for you." Margaret placed the ring box in Randall's hand.

He crumpled his brows together in puzzlement as he looked down at the box. "What is this?"

"Open it."

Randall followed Margaret's instructions and opened the delicate velvet box. Inside was a magnificent topaz and diamond ring. "Where did you get this?" Randall asked.

"It was our grandmother's ring. Father gave it to me when I turned thirteen. I want you to have it and propose to Jackie with it. You both deserve it."

"It's superb, Margaret, but I cannot take it."

"Why ever not?"

"Because Father gave it to you."

"He gave everything to me because you were not around to give anything to at the time. You would have been given some of the family heirlooms to pass down to your family. He would want you to have this, as do I."

"Thank you, Maggie. Jacquelyn will love this ring."

"I know. I am glad you can give it to her."

"Indeed. Can you believe that soon, we will both be happily married?"

Margaret knew it would be true for him, but she worried she would never feel happiness again.

❧

Margaret was reading in the library when Jackie and Randall surged into the room. "We did it."

Startled, Margaret glanced up to find the couple grinning and radiating delight. "Let me see it, let me see the ring."

Jackie rushed over to Margaret and pushed her hand out to her friend. Margaret took it in her own and inspected the topaz ring. It looked perfect on her hand.

Not wanting to spoil it by explaining she had already seen it, she kept the information to herself. "You did brilliant, Randall. It is a magnificent engagement ring."

"He did, did he not? Did you know it was a family ring, your grandmother's ring, to be exact? But it is not an engagement ring, Maggie."

"What do you mean 'it is not an engagement ring'? I am looking right at it."

"This is my wedding ring. We could not wait and decided to elope."

Elope? Did she hear Jackie, right? They were already married? Margaret dropped Jackie's hand and asked, "You got married without me there?"

Randall sat down next to Margaret on the window seat. "Do not be upset. We still plan to have a reception with everyone we care about, especially you."

Margaret was in disbelief. She wanted to be pleased for them, but she had barely processed her brother telling her he was in love with Jackie, and now she had to rapidly accept their choice to secretly get married. She had assumed they would be getting married after her and Michel had their wedding, not before.

"Congratulations to both of you," Margaret said in a flat tone.

"Do you think you can muster a little bit more enthusiasm, dear sister?"

"You two love each other and you got married. I am glad for you."

"What is wrong?"

"Nothing. I am just adjusting. It is a lot to process."

"Maggie, you—" Before he could finish, a piercing scream of terror interrupted their conversation.

Margaret jumped from the shock of it as chills raced up and down her spine, then realized that it was her son's panicked cries. "Oh my goodness, that was Henry!" She grabbed her skirts and ran towards his room, Randall following close behind. She flung open the door and rushed over to his crib.

She grabbed him up, asking, "What? What is it, my darling?"

Still crying and shaking with fear, her son pointed to the window and said, "Bad man."

She looked at her son who had been picking up more words lately, almost at a startling pace. She realized he must have had a bad dream and thought someone had come in through the window.

Several of the servants rushed in, still pulling on robes and slippers.

"My lady, is the boy all right?" Albert asked, holding a lantern in one shaking hand and a pistol that looked almost as old as him in the other.

"Yes, I think he had a bad dream. You may all go back to sleep. I will stay with him."

They looked to Randall for his approval. They were already viewing him as the head of the home as the Earl of Renwick, Margaret realized. At first it had upset her, since she had always been the one in charge, but it was his rightful place to be their master. Knowing that, she amended her attitude to them looking to him as the authority around their home and became accustomed to it, since it should have been his role all along.

Randall nodded and said, "I will stay with them as well."

The assembled servants left one by one, whispering about the boy's first nightmare and what might have caused it. She also wondered what had brought this on. It was probably just all the craziness that had been going on lately. First Francisca and, then more recently, Motty left the family's service. He had a new uncle, and soon he would have a new father. It was a lot of change for anyone, especially a little boy who did not know how to process it all. Perhaps she needed to take him away for a while. Well, they would all be leaving soon enough after the wedding for an extended trip to Portugal.

"Is Albert getting senile in his old age?"

Margaret looked at Randall in puzzlement. "Whatever motivated that question?"

"I just find it odd that he would rush into the room with a loaded pistol when all Henry did was cry out in his sleep."

How could she answer that? To her, it was perfectly normal for Albert to react the way he did, considering he worried that Catherine or the duke would one day find them. He always kept a pistol close at hand, just in case they ever needed it.

Choosing to avoid answering the question directly, she said, "You know he is extremely protective over Henry."

Henry was still sobbing and Margaret sat down in the rocking chair to calm him down. "Oh, darling, it is all right. Mummy is here, and I will stay with you. I will not let anything or anyone hurt you."

She held him for several minutes as he calmed down. She went to put him back in his crib, but he started to cry again.

"All right, I suppose you can sleep with me tonight."

He curled against her and rested his head in the crook of her neck. She patted and rubbed his back lightly as she headed for the door.

She stopped and turned to face Randall. "Are you coming?"

"I will be there in a minute," he said as he walked over to the window.

"Good night, then. I will see you in the morning."

"Good night, Maggie."

CHAPTER 24

*D*eciding to go riding again, Margaret invited Randall to travel to the stables with her. He agreed, admitting he was thinking of purchasing a horse for Jackie as a wedding gift. Not one for riding, as Jackie was not one for pleasure riding, but one they could enter as a contestant in racing. Jackie loved anything she could bet on, so Randall thought it would be the perfect gift.

When Charlie saw Margaret, she neighed and threw her mane back in happiness. Margaret walked up to her horse and patted her coat, talking to her affectionately.

"I am so glad that you are here. I have missed you so much. I promise that I will never leave you again. I do not care what it takes to keep you with me."

She had just mounted Charlie when Randall walked up, asking, "Where are you going riding?"

"I think I will take the paths to the east this time. I have already explored the other areas."

Randall approached Charlie and rubbed her down for a few moments, then looked up and asked his sister, "Last time we were here, I forgot to ask you, why did you not send for your horse?"

Avoiding the whole truth, Margaret answered evasively, "Because, when our father died, he passed away with a mountain of debt. The estate was taken over, and I lost everything. That is why I came here."

"Yes, I understand that, but what happened to everything your husband owned?"

Trying to sidestep the question, she said, "It is such a lovely day for a ride. Would you like to join me?"

"Yes, in a moment, but you still have not answered my question. Between what happened last night with Henry and all the times you have evaded answering my questions, I feel like you have been keeping things from me. I think it is time you tell me the truth about what happened back in England."

She wrinkled her face in thought. What would be the easiest thing to do? She knew she could not tell him every-thing. She did not want to relive the memories again, so instead she said, "He did not trust me before he died and he left everything to his sister." She pressed her lips together. "There, are you satisfied?"

"I am sorry. I did not know. I thought you had loved each other."

She pulled in on the reins to keep Charlie from shuffling her feet. Her horse could feel the tension in her.

"I did and still do love him, and he had loved me... up until the end."

"What happened, I mean, to change his feelings?"

"I would rather not talk about it."

"But I only ask because what happened seems to upset you and—"

Margaret did not let him finish his thoughts, but interrupted him instead. "What happened back then does not matter. And I have changed my mind. I think I would much rather ride by myself. I will be back in an hour or so."

With that, she turned Charlie around and galloped off, leaving Randall to watch their departing figures.

She hated treating Randall like that. She hated that she could not think about her husband without sadness flooding her. But most of all, she hated the power that Witherton and Catherine still had over her.

Catherine she feared because she wanted to take her son away, and it was a mother's instinct to hate any danger to her child. But she was afraid of Witherton for a completely different reason. She feared him because, every time she thought of him, she thought about what he had done to her.

Without wanting them to, the memories of that horrible night would still descend on her and haunt her. Sometimes, too often to mention, she would wake up in the dead of the night sweating from her nightmares. And every day, she fought back the fear that one day he would find her.

Looking for a place to rest, Margaret noticed an area in front of her, which looked to be a lake. She slowed Charlie down as they approached it, finally bringing her horse to a stop. Dismounting, she walked over to the lake. She stood and stared at it for several minutes. It looked a great deal like the lake that she and Henry had spent time in right before his death. She had been so happy back then.

Margaret sat down and slowly made trails in the water's edge with her fingers as she permitted herself for the first time in a long time to think about everything going on in her life.

Yes, she was happy, but it was happiness she felt for others, not for herself. She felt merely contentment for herself, and mild contentment at that. In large part, it was due to her relationship, or rather lack of relationship with Michel. She knew she did not love Michel the way she should, but she felt she had no other choice but to marry him. If she did not follow through and commit to him, it would not only cost her own future, but her entire family's as well.

Standing up, Margaret walked over to a nearby tree. She leaned against it and sighed. How did she get here? Everything was so complicated now. Her life had been so simple when she was younger, and now nothing made sense. Nothing had in a long time.

She was staring at the water when she heard a noise from behind. Thinking it was Randall, she said, "Rand, even though I asked to be alone, I am glad that you came after me. I have some things I need to tell you."

Hearing another noise from the same direction, Margaret turned her head, expecting to see her brother. But instead, what she saw made her lose her breath and sway in terror. Without thinking, she turned and started to run, not caring where she went except away from *him*.

But with only a few quick strides, Witherton caught up with her and grabbed her arm, saying in his cold, cruel voice, "I told you that you would never escape me, Margaret."

She tried to break free from his grasp, but his grip only became firmer. He towered over her as he snapped, "You are not getting away, so you might as well stop fighting me."

Realizing he was right, at least for the moment, she did as he said and stopped squirming. With shock in her voice, Margaret asked, "How did you find me?"

He looked down at her with his cruel, blue eyes. "I have to admit, you have been clever, little one. Tracking you down has proved most difficult. But as you know, I never give up on something I want. I did not care how many men or how much money it took. You were never going to escape me." He laughed triumphantly. "You really should be more careful about whom you trust. One of my detectives overheard an admirer of yours, some Frenchman I believe, talking about you in an English pub." He smiled maliciously. "Once I knew you were in France, it was simple enough to locate you."

Margaret glared up at him in anger. Then lowered her head, disgusted with the look of conquest he had on his face.

He had found her. Pierre had stupidly given her away without knowing it because he was still so obsessed with her that he could not control talking about her.

It was never going to end. She was never going to be able to escape Witherton or what happened.

"I have seen the child, and I know he is my son."

Her head jerked up in horror. She tried to mask her fear before saying, "I do not know what you are talking about."

"The boy at your new estate, the one you claim is Rolantry's heir. You will not be able to pass him off as that much longer. My traits are already starting to take over."

It dawned on her that he must have been the one her son had seen in his room the other night. He had seen him, most probably touched him. Oh my God, he could have taken him!

Even more fear took siege as she stuttered out, "You... you are wrong. He is Henry's son. He carries his name as well as his blood in his veins."

"You would like to think that, but I will let you in on a little secret. Henry was sterile. He could not father a child even if he had wanted to."

She narrowed her eyes in hate and disbelief. "You are lying."

"No, you see, I was the one who caused the accident that took away his ability to father children. Of course, the doctors said there was a *slight* chance that he *might* be able to someday, although they told him not to put any wager on it. Of course, I, on the other hand, am quite virile, as you well know," he said, leering at her with a provocative grin.

He rubbed her cheek with his free hand, and instinctively, she recoiled.

"Come, come now, you do not think that I would do anything to you right here in the open?"

"I would not put it past you."

"I only came here to make a proposal to you. Actually, you really have no choice but to accept it. Once you hear it, you will understand what I mean by that." He let her go. "And do not even think about running away. If you try, I promise you will regret it."

She stood her ground but kept her eyes open for anything that could help her escape. She waited what seemed forever while he continuously watched her like a lion stalking its prey. Then finally, he said, "I want you and I want my son. You will be my mistress, and he will have a good education and be taken care of for the rest of his life."

She gripped her fists at her sides and forced herself not to slap him.

"I told you once that I would never become your mistress. I still stand by that."

He growled with the fury that she saw rising in him. "Have it your way. I want you both badly enough that I will make the sacrifice to marry you and take the boy as my heir." Arrogantly, thinking he had offered something of great value, he added, "You surely cannot object to that."

She swayed in shock. She never thought he would propose marriage to her after their last confrontation. It had been so horrible, and he had basically used her and discarded her to get at her husband.

"Why? You made it clear back in England that you only used me to hurt Henry."

"I want you. I have always wanted you. And I want the boy. I told you I would do whatever it takes to have you both."

She raised her chin and said defiantly, "No."

"No? What do you mean 'no'?"

"Exactly that. I will *never* be yours. I am engaged to the Marquis de Badour, and I will be marrying him next week."

Biting each word out in anger, he said with spitefulness, "Perhaps I need to give you more incentive. Let me explain the circumstances to you. Catherine is looking for you—actually, for your son. She could not care less about you. Up until now, she has had no luck and cannot seem to locate you, thanks to me. But one flick of my wrist, one letter from me, and she will know where you are and will come and take your son."

She narrowed her eyes, trying to hide the fear his words invoked. "I said never, and I meant it. I hate you! Just the thought of you touching me makes me sick. I hate even looking at you."

Without her even knowing what happened, he reached out and grabbed her arms, yanking her towards him.

He glared down into her eyes. "You are walking a fine line, my dear. I thought I had broken your irritating pride the last time. Must I do it again?"

She shrank back. "If you try, I will kill you!"

He laughed sadistically. "You threatened that before, but here I stand, quite alive. We will see if you can muster up the strength to carry out your threats."

With that, he threw her on the ground so hard it knocked the air from her lungs. She gasped, trying to block out the pain. She was not going to let this happen again.

She started wiggling, trying to get free, but he leaned down on top of her. He whispered in her ear, "I thought you had already learned your lesson about defying me, but I see that I must teach you again. Perhaps you will remember the next time."

Margaret was starting to panic. If she did not get free soon, it would be too late to stop him. She barely made it through the last time he violated her; she did not think she could survive it a second time.

She began to cry out, begging anyone who was around to help her. She was so intent on trying to get someone's attention, she had not been aware of what he was doing. By the time she realized he was pushing up her skirts, the degradation and crudity of the situation made her recoil. The thought of how close he was to her bare skin made her start screaming even louder as she kicked and twisted underneath his weight.

Angry at her defiance, the duke pulled back his hand and hit her across the face. The blow sent her reeling, and she could barely focus enough to breath.

"I told you to stop fighting me, little one. This will be easier for you if you just give in and enjoy it."

Terror began to take hold of Margaret. The longer she went without being able to get away from him, the deeper the fear gripped her. Unable to free herself, she began to pray to God. *Lord, please help me. I cannot go through this again. I need your help. Please, God, please, help me!*

As he straddled her and started to fumble with his belt, Margaret reached out and searched for anything that could help. Her hand came in contact with a jagged rock. She grabbed it and, without thinking, swung up and over.

She heard a loud crack, and then Witherton slumped forward onto her. She laid on the dewy grass for several seconds as she tried to catch her breath. Still shaken from his attack, she forced herself to focus on pushing him off. She heard him groan as she rolled his body away. Margaret knew she had to move quickly as possible before he had a chance to wake up, knowing that once he did, he was going to come after her with a vengeance.

Off balance and disoriented, she rushed towards where she thought she had left her horse. Not finding her, Margaret leaned against a tree and whistled for Charlie. Across the clearing, from behind a bunch of trees, her horse came forward. She mounted without a backwards glance and galloped towards the stables.

She had to get Henry and hide. If Witherton found her, or worse yet, told Catherine where they were like he threatened, she would lose everything. When she reached the stables, she dismounted and hurriedly handed the reins over to the stable boy, who was stunned to see her come back splattered with blood.

Fear guided her as she rushed towards the carriage house, thinking only of fleeing. But before she could escape, Randall found her. He stopped her fleeing figure with his nonchalant voice. "Where are you going in such a hurry? Did you forget about me?"

Margaret stopped without turning around or saying a word.

Not realizing the gravity of his sister's situation and only noticing the muddled state she appeared to be in, he asked, "What happened on your ride? Did your horse throw you?"

She turned her head to face him, and he must have seen the red mark that was sure to stand out against her pale skin.

He reached out and touched her cheek lightly, causing Margaret to shrink away in distress.

"If Michel did that to you, I swear I will kill him."

Mechanically, she lifted her hand to push back her hair that had fallen free from her bun during the attack. Randall watched her, and his eyes fell to the blood that was on her sleeve. He grabbed her arm and pulled her around to face him.

Startled by the blood that was still wet and all over her yellow and tan riding habit, he asked, "What happened out there, Maggie? Why are you covered in blood?"

She glanced down in dismay. Disconcerted, she whimpered, twisting free from his grasp.

Margaret took a few steps back and gazed with an unfocused look over his shoulder. She stood there for several moments before she started backing up and then quickly turned around, trying to flee. But he grabbed her again before she could get away.

"Where is he? Where is Michel? I will teach him never to hit a woman again."

Her head snapped up and her eyes finally focused. She glared at him, saying, "Michel had nothing to do with what happened to me."

"Then whose blood is all over your clothes?"

She pressed her lips together, not wanting to talk about the violent attack that had just been inflicted on her.

He shook her, not thinking what effect it would have on her. "Tell me. If I am going to help you, I need to know what happened."

She cried out from fear, and he released her as quickly as if he had been holding a flame.

He dropped his balled fists to his sides and then asked again, "What happened while you were riding, Margaret?"

"*He* found us." She looked up at her brother and whispered, "Rand, is that you?" And before she knew what was happening, Margaret was falling as her brother caught her collapsing body.

CHAPTER 25

*O*pening her eyes, Margaret tried to focus her vision. Everything was blurry and her head was pounding. "What... what is going on?"

"You fainted earlier today after you came home from riding."

She looked to the side and found Randall sitting next to her. She reached out to him and said, "I feel horrible, Rand. My whole body hurts and I—"

Oh, my goodness, Witherton! I have to get Henry and get out of here. Nothing else matters. She sat up quickly, too quickly, and grabbed her head.

"Lie back down, Maggie. You need to rest. We can talk about what happened later." He patted her hand and then stood up. "I will leave you to rest. You are safe now, in your chambers."

Margaret pretended to fall back asleep and forced herself

to wait until he left the room. Once she heard the click of the door, Margaret jumped up.

She was shaking with fear but paused only long enough to adjust to the pain all over her body. She headed for her closet and reached in to drag out a trunk, already packed with the bare minimum she needed. She took out a second one that was packed with Henry's belongings. She had kept them both ready, part of her knowing this time would eventually come.

Running over to her vanity, Margaret grabbed her jewelry box. She would need all of it to sell once their money ran out. Unlocking another drawer, she pulled out a billfold full of money. It was not much, but it would help.

She was putting them with her other things when Randall walked in. She stopped midaction, bent over her trunk.

He looked from her to the trunk and back to her with a scowl on his face. "What is going on?"

"I am packing. What does it look like?"

"I can see that, but why?"

Straightening up, Margaret grimaced in pain. Not looking at him, she replied, "Because I am leaving France, and I am taking Henry with me. I will contact you as soon as it is safe." She looked at her brother with fear and desperation. "I do not want to leave you, Rand, but I must," she said, trying to keep the tears from falling.

She bent down and continued packing, thinking there was nothing left to say. Apparently, she was wrong, as

Randall walked over to her and pulled her around. "I want to help you, Maggie, but you keep everything from me. Let me in, let me help you. You have to tell me what is going on."

Margaret started to object out of hand but, after a moment's hesitation, decided she loved her brother enough to at least tell him why she was leaving France. She wanted him to understand and not think she was deserting him. It was bad enough that both Michel and Jackie were going to think that.

"I suppose you are right." She walked over and sat at the windowsill. She needed its comfort in order to be able to get through telling him everything.

"I told you I was married, but I have never told you much more than that. Our father betrothed me to Henry when I was only a child."

"I remember Henry and your betrothal to him."

Margaret nodded, then continued, "I thought I did not love him and that I was in love with another man. His name was Richard Charles Crawley III, the Duke of Witherton, and he was dashing, charming, and suave. And he was also Henry's most bitter enemy. I thought he really loved me, and when he asked our father for my hand in marriage, and Father said no, I thought I could not live without him.

"Father would not compromise his choice in marriage for me and made me wed Henry. At first, I let my feelings for the duke cloud my marriage with Henry." She turned and looked at her brother. "I never acted on it, my honor would not allow that, but I continued to yearn for him in secret.

"Over time, Henry made me understand what I really felt for Witherton was nothing more than infatuation, that there was no substance there. Henry made me realize that he was not only my best friend but also my one true love.

"So I told Witherton that he needed to leave me be and move on, but he continued to pursue me. Of course, it made Henry seethe with jealousy because he did not believe me when I told him that I no longer wanted to be with Witherton. Then things took a turn for the worst. Witherton sent me a note telling me that he had damaging information regarding Henry, and if I did not come to see him, he would release it to the newspapers."

She shook her head in sadness. "I look back now, and I realize what a fool I was to fall into his trap. He had been setting me up all along, you see. But my only thoughts were of saving Henry from a scandal. So, I went to his estate, and he... he—" Her voice cracked. She could not get the words past her lips. Unshed tears were in the back of her throat, keeping her from being able to finish.

Not that she wanted to anyway. Margaret hated saying what he did to her, because what happened to her that night held so much shame, guilt, and pain that sometimes it threatened to overwhelm her and sink her into a pit of despair. She felt so dirty just thinking about it that the thought of saying the words made her shiver with disgust. She was trying to hold back the tears, but they pushed past anyway. And her crying, which was soft at first, turned into great racking sobs that shook her whole body.

Randall walked over and took her in his arms. "Mags, it is all right. You do not have to finish."

She hiccupped and shook her head. "No, I need to say this. I need you to know what happened to me."

She brushed at the tears on her face and leaned her head on her brother's shoulder, then continued from where she left off. "He threw me to the ground and he forced me. He used me, and then he left me lying on the floor." Margaret heard Randall mumble some curses under his breath and felt his grip tighten from anger.

"But the worst part of all was that he had planned it. He told Henry that I would be there and that he would see my 'true nature.' When Henry got there, I was so in shock that I did everything wrong. Henry did not believe me when I told him that Witherton had... had forced himself on me and compromised me without my consent.

"Henry banished me to our London estate." She gritted her teeth in anger. "He told me he never wanted to see me again, and then he challenged Witherton to a duel over my honor. He left me standing there to face that beast all alone. He left me, and I never saw him again."

Margaret paused for several seconds, trying to bring her emotions under control. "He was killed in their duel over me, and he never knew that I carried his child." Not wanting Randall to question her statement, she swiftly stated, "And I *know* Henry is my husband's son."

She looked up at her brother and wanted him to understand. "I fled to France to escape Henry's sister, Catherine, who planned to take Henry away and raise him without me in his life, since he was the Rolantry heir. I also left to escape Witherton, who Catherine threatened to tell and had vowed he would make me his mistress, despite my bitter protests.

"I thought I was safe, that I was going to be able to start over, but today, Witherton found me. He said that he had seen Henry. He was in his room, Rand. He could have taken him and I never would have been able to find him. But what I did not know is that he also came for me. He told me he wanted me as his mistress, and when I said no, he offered to marry me. When I still refused, he threatened to tell Catherine where Henry and I are.

"And when I still refused, he hit me and tried to... he tried to force me again. But I screamed and I screamed, and then I found a rock and I hit him. I hit him, and I heard this crack, and blood splattered, and I ran. I just ran until Charlie found me, and then I kept thinking.... I was so scared, Rand. If he comes back here...." She started to cry again.

"Maggie, I am here, and I swear that I will not let him get near you ever again. I wish I had been there. I swear I would have killed the bloody bastard myself! I cannot believe you have been holding all of this inside you. I wondered sometimes, when you would get this sad, distant look, what you were thinking about, and now it all makes sense." Then, almost as if the complex puzzle was finally solved, Randall blurted out, "That night you found me and you were taken by those men, this Witherton person sent them."

"Yes. I should have left France that night, but I had just

found you and, foolishly, I thought I could have Monsieur Mulchere give him false information to get him to stop looking for me here." Margaret shook her head with regret. "There is no escaping him, not as long as I stay where he has all the power."

He looked down into her eyes and said, "It will be all right, and when I tell Michel, he will take care of everything."

"No. He does not need to know. We are leaving tomorrow, and he need never know."

"But why?"

"I am disgraced, do you not see that?"

"No, you were violated. Another man took you without your consent. That is not your fault."

"But according to Witherton and Catherine, I willingly allowed it to happen, and who will everyone believe?"

Randall said nothing, but his frown was all she needed. "The look on your face confirms what I have known all along. If anyone in French society finds out about what happened to me, I will be ruined. Now you see why I must leave and not tell Michel that Witherton has found me. He will only try to stop me, and it will be better this way. He will not have to face the scandal that is tied to my past. I thought I had escaped it, that it had been covered up, but one word from Witherton and I will be destroyed. I could not face Michel like that."

"All right, if this is how you want it, but I am coming with you."

"And so am I."

Both of them turned, shocked to hear someone interrupt their private conversation. At the door stood Jackie.

"How long have you been there?" Margaret asked defensively.

"Long enough to catch the basic gist of things."

Margaret, a bit angry from having someone else hear about her tainted past, glared at her friend for several seconds. Haughtily, she said to Jackie, "You would never make it where I am going."

Jackie laughed, breaking the somberness of the whole situation. "Mon chéri, you have no idea what I can withstand."

"Yes, I am sure you have had your share of 'interesting' situations and have been to quite a few different places with your lovers, but where I am going, no one will want to go."

Randall furrowed his brows together and asked, "What place could be that horrible?"

Margaret frowned with disdain and said, "The Americas."

"Why would we go to that distasteful place?" Randall asked, clearly repulsed by the idea.

"Since our future is there. Father secretly left land deeded to me. I was unaware of it until he passed away, but I checked his secret hiding place under the floorboard in his study. Afraid the debt collectors would take it, I hid it for safekeeping. When Henry died, it was the only thing I had that I knew Catherine could not take from me because no one knew I had it.

"It finally makes sense to me now. I believe God had

Father make those arrangements so we would have a new start and be able to make a new home for ourselves. It would be the only place Witherton and Catherine would not think to look for us."

"And rightly so, as no one in their right mind would want to go there."

"You should make peace with it, Rand. Come tomorrow, we will leave Europe forever."

CHAPTER 26

hen Margaret told Alfred and Sarah that the family would be leaving Europe, they had asked to join them. She had explained that it was going to be a difficult journey in an unfamiliar place with no pay until they reached their destination. It did not deter them from choosing to go with them, even after she explained that it was America.

"That is the last of the luggage, my lady," Alfred stated as the carriage driver lifted down the final trunk and placed it on the docks.

Margaret took in their surroundings and found herself drawn to the enormous ship just a few feet away. She had never been on a vessel so gigantic, nor been on such a lengthy voyage. It made her apprehensive just thinking about it, but she knew she needed to remain calm for her son's sake. She could feel his tiny hand in her own, and she knew that if she showed any fear, he would sense it and become frightened as well. As always, his well-being was her utmost concern.

Jackie sighed loudly, making sure both Margaret and Randall heard it, and then stated in an irritated manner, "I hope they allow us to board shortly. I am tepid and exhausted, and I want to lie down in my stateroom."

Margaret smiled in amusement at Jackie's exaggerated demeanor. Trying not to frustrate her further, Margaret faked a serious tone. "I am sure it will not be much longer, Jackie. They just need to finish loading the second-class passengers, and then they will be ready to allow us to board."

Fortunately, Margaret had been preparing financially for this day by stashing away enough money to secure all of them first-class accommodations while they crossed the Atlantic. Secretly, she had always known that her past would catch up with her; it was just a matter of when it happened. That time had finally come, and she was glad she had made it a priority not to be stuck without any way to escape because of money.

Together with her toddler son, Randall, Jackie, and her two loyal servants, Albert and Sarah, she was going to forge a new path.

Margaret patted the pocket of her skirt and made sure the papers that secured their futures were safe. When the family estate had been impoverished due to her father's illness and death, everything had been sold to pay off as much debt as possible. But the collectors did not find the secret spot that was hidden beneath the floorboards in her father's study. God had given her a way out, provided her with a means of escape for something that had not happened yet. God often worked in ways she did not understand but were always best for her.

Instinctively, it had been the first place that Margaret had looked after everything had been taken away. They had given her the day to finish collecting their personal items before they took the manor as well. When she had removed the floorboards, she was surprised to find not one but two boxes. She had pulled them out and remembered her father had privately given her a key on her sixteenth birthday. When she tried it on the boxes, one opened. What she found inside was a deed to a piece of land in America, a large amount of money, and a second key.

The second box held another key and a note saying that it opened a safety deposit box at the bank in Boulder City, Colorado. She took the deed, money, and safety deposit key and tucked them away for safekeeping. She never told Henry about it because, well, she wanted something that was her own, and if she were honest with herself, she did not ever completely trust him. Now, as she thought about it, she realized that even back then, somehow part of her new that things were bound to go wrong because he had never been secure in their relationship. He was always testing her, trying to prove her loyalty was real.

She was going to claim their land in America and find out

what was in that deposit box. She hoped it was enough to start a new life.

Randall jolted Margaret out of her thoughts by asking, "Maggie, you are standing firm in your decision not to tell Michel we are leaving?"

"Yes, as I told you, once he knows what happened, he will try to intervene and all the sordid details of my past will come out. I will be ruined and his reputation will be tarnished by even bigger scandal than by me quietly leaving France. I do not want to do that to him, and I would rather not destroy him when I know we do not have a future together anyway."

"I think you are making a mistake. He might surprise you, and you are not even giving him a chance."

"I do not have the luxury of giving anyone a chance. Witherton has made that impossible."

"Stop bothering her about her decision, Rand. She is capable of making her own choices," Jackie inserted.

"I know she is, but I would not be a very good brother if I did not point out—"

Margaret interrupted them both, hoping to avoid a fight and not wanting to think about how hard it was to have to leave everything behind for a second time. "It is all right, truly. We do not need to discuss this any further."

Both of them looked away sheepishly, as if realizing that they had made a hard situation more difficult.

"I am sorry, Mags. I did not mean to make this more

painful." Randall gently put his hand on his sister's shoulder and rubbed it.

"Me too, Margaret. Please forgive us. We were not being considerate."

"No need to apologize. We just need to focus on moving forward."

Margaret corrected her hat on top of her head and smoothed out the wrinkles in her outfit in preparation for boarding. She watched as the last of the second-class passengers were getting on the ship.

As she started to move towards the ocean liner, she heard a carriage pull up behind her and someone shout, "Margaret, wait."

Margaret froze. She recognized the voice immediately. It was Michel. What was he doing there? She had thought she would be able to get away without having to deal with ending their relationship in person. She had given a letter to Sarah to deliver right before it was time to leave. She had not considered the possibility that he would be able to get to her before she was on board the ship.

She felt a hand on her arm pulling her firmly around, and she found herself face-to-face with her soon-to-be ex-fiancé. "What are you doing here?" Margaret asked cautiously.

Michel pulled out a piece of paper from his jacket pocket with his free hand and waved it at her. "I came here to find out why you are really leaving. You do not expect me to believe the ridiculous explanation you wrote in this letter as to why you are abandoning your promise to marry me."

Margaret looked up at Michel and could see the hurt in his eyes. She hated that her actions caused it and even more that she was not able to fully explain what was going on.

"The letter perfectly clarifies why I am leaving France. I have matters to attend to back in England. Matters that will not afford me the latitude to return to France, and therefore, I cannot marry you, Michel."

"Nonsense. I do not believe a word of what you are saying. If you need to deal with anything in England, I can go with you and help you take care of it."

"What about your sister?"

"I can have my brother and the servants watch after her while I am temporarily away. Granted, she is my responsibility, but it is also my job as your betrothed to take care of you and your family."

And there it was, what Margaret had been afraid of all along. She knew that he would not let her go without a fight. She did not want to have to tell him about the duke's latest attack, but it was beginning to look like she might not have any other choice.

"I did not want you to have to get involved, Michel. This problem stems from a long time ago, and it is my mess to clean up."

"I want to help you, Margaret. All you have to do is let me."

"Why do you keep persisting in this? I do not want to make this any more difficult than it already has to be."

"You leaving me, Margaret, cannot be made easy. No matter how hard you try, it will not be painless."

And deep down she knew Michel was right. She had been avoiding the truth for a long time now, but she did have feelings for him, more than she cared to acknowledge.

"Why will you not open up to me, Margaret? Something has happened since the last time I saw you, and you are not telling me. I know it has something to do with your past."

Margaret averted her eyes and replied in a veiled tone, "I do not know what you mean."

"I think you do, but I think you have become so accustomed to keeping secrets that you are uncomfortable sharing them with anyone."

"I told you, Michel, I came to France to search for my brother, and I found him. End of story. Now that my business in France is done, it is time for me to return to England."

"But you fled England. What has changed that has allowed you to return?"

Margaret glanced at the ship behind her and realized that she needed to be boarding soon or there was a chance it might take off without them.

"I have to go. I do not have time for this. The ship will leave without us."

"You mean the ship headed for America? How is it, if you need to be back in England, that you are about to board a ship destined for America?"

Margaret winced, realizing that Michel was too smart for both their goods.

"Quit lying to me, Margaret." He lightly grabbed her by the shoulders and pleaded, "Tell me the truth."

Margaret hung her head in humiliation and whispered dejectedly, "I do not want to, Michel. I am too ashamed."

"Do not be, Margaret. I already know about your past and I accept you. I care for you more than you can possibly know. You can tell me anything. There is nothing you can say that will drive me away."

Still staring down at the ground, unable to muster the strength to look Michel in the eyes, Margaret said softly, "I was desperate and the only choice I had was to run. It seems I am in the same position once more."

"Please, tell me what is going on so I can help you."

"There is nothing anyone can do."

"You are wrong. There is something you need to know. When Pierre came and told me the private details regarding your past, I could not propose to you without talking with you about it first, which is why I decided to discuss it with you at the park. I believed what you told me, but I also knew if it ever came out, we would need to have evidence to back up your claims to protect you from ruination. I had a couple of my investigators dig deeper into the details, and that is when they found conflicting reports from several of the servants who worked for your family, but have since been dismissed. They confirmed your account of the events from that night. One even received a note from the duke addressed to you. The proof from their testimonies confirmed you were not the guilty party and you had been the casualty of a horrible atrocity."

Michel put his hand under Margaret's chin and lifted her face so that their eyes could meet. "And after getting to know you and who you are as a person, I was certain that you were not to blame. You are a good and honorable woman, Margaret, and I hate that you have been made to feel ashamed of your past."

He leaned down and gently kissed her on the lips. He whispered, "You never have to feel that way with me. I love you, not in spite of your past but *because* of your past. It is what has made you who you are, and I love everything about you."

Suddenly a floodgate of tears unleashed from Margaret; she did not even realize she had been holding them back. She leaned into Michel and rested her cheek on his chest as he wrapped his arms around her. She had waited so long to hear him say he loved her, and now when she had to leave, he finally said it. It was not fair. How was she going to leave him?

After several moments, Margaret forced herself to pull away from Michel's embrace and step back, trying to distance herself and steel herself for what came next.

"I still have to leave, Michel."

"No, you do not. Whatever is going on, we can handle it together."

"We cannot. He will stop at nothing to take my son and destroy me in the process."

"You are referring to the Duke of Witherton, I presume?"

"Yes, he was here. He stalked my son, as well as attacked and threatened me. I barely got away this time, and when he finds me again, my life will be over."

"I can shield you, all of you, from him."

Margaret looked up at her fiancé and realized he believed what he was saying. But she knew the duke far better than anyone, and she knew how he operated. There was no protection from him, only running and hiding. Anonymity would be her only true defense, because the duke would obliterate anyone who got in his way.

"I cannot ask that of you, Michel. I want to stay and marry you, but I will not risk your life to save my own."

"I have no life without you, Margaret. I need you."

"Why has it taken you this long to tell me how you feel? I have waited so long to hear you say you love and need me."

"Truthfully, it was when I got your letter and read it that I realized how deeply I felt. The thought of losing you made me face my own feelings and admit how much I truly love you."

And Margaret realized that she loved him too. She had been pushing the feeling aside, blaming his lack of emotion, but she had been holding back, secretly dreading the moment that she feared would come and shatter what they had. But here it was, and they were both still standing— together. She did not have to be afraid anymore.

"I love you too."

"Then you will stay. You will come home with me, and we will get married immediately so that you can stay with me in my home. We can have a formal celebration down the road, but your family's safety is of paramount importance, and to guarantee that, you need to be living with me."

"I agree."

Michel gestured to several of the dock workers and said, "Please load Lady Margaret's and her family's baggage back onto their carriage. They have had a change of plans and will not be traveling today."

Randall walked over and stated, "I take it from the luggage being put back on our carriage that we will not be going to the Americas after all?"

Margaret shook her head. "It seems that I will be getting married this evening instead."

Jackie and Randall smiled enthusiastically. "That is the best news I have heard in a long while," Randall exclaimed.

The best friends hugged and Jackie laughed, saying, "We are both going to be newlyweds by day's end."

Michel led Margaret over to his carriage. "Let us head home in my carriage, Margaret. Randall, Jackie, and the rest of your family can follow in yours."

He helped her up and then gracefully climbed in next to her. He tapped the side of the carriage door to let the driver know they were ready to leave. Quickly, the carriage took off down the cobblestone road.

"When we get home, I will send for a justice of the court,

and we will be married before night's end. Are you ready to be my wife?"

"Yes, Michel, I want nothing more than for us to be man and wife."

Giddily, Margaret leaned over and kissed Michel, who fervently kissed her back. She could not believe that, just moments ago, she had been trying to convince herself to walk away from this man forever. She loved him so much she could barely contain it. Leaving him behind would have been the worst mistake of her life.

"I love you, Michel. I love you so much.'

"I love you too, Margaret. You make me so happy. I should have told you a long time ago."

Wrapping her arms around his neck, she gently pulled him close. "I cannot wait until tonight, *after* we say our vows and we *actually* become man and wife."

"Believe me, I have thought about it as well, and nothing will please me more than to claim you as my wife in our marriage bed." He leaned in and kissed her again, deeper and fuller that time, allowing his lips to linger on hers as he gently caressed the small of her back and slowly pulled her in against his lengthy frame. "Margaret," he groaned against her lips, causing his breath to tickle her skin. She purred at the sound of her name and snuggled even further into his embrace. "Margaret." That time it sounded almost as a plea, and she realized they were on the brink of no return. If they continued, they would not make it to their wedding night.

Margaret reluctantly pulled away. "Only a few more hours and we will never have to stop again."

He smiled seductively and whispered, "I do not want to stop."

She blushed and then replied candidly, "I do not want to either."

With that, he grabbed her around the waist and yanked her to him again, smothering her in ardent kisses. Giddy and spinning from the intoxication of their passion, Margaret could hardly focus on anything else, but abruptly, she felt the carriage come to a halt. Mid-embrace, both Margaret and Michel looked around. Something did not feel right. Margaret did not know why, but she was sure something was wrong.

"Michel, I am scared. Why have we stopped? It is too soon for us to be home."

"I know," he said in a steely tone. She felt his body stiffen as his hand immediately went to the sword at his waist.

Michel leaned towards the window and looked out. He furrowed his eyebrows together in frustration. "I cannot see anything. I need to get out so that I can ask the driver why we are not still moving."

Margaret grabbed Michel's arm. "Do not leave me. I do not want to be left alone in here."

"You need not worry. The carriage probably has a wheel that has come loose and they stopped to fix it before it came off completely." He leaned towards Margaret and kissed her on the lips. "Wait here. I will be right back."

Before Margaret could say another word, Michel jumped out of the carriage. Moments ticked by and nothing happened, making her even more anxious. What was taking so long?

She moved towards the window and gazed out, trying to locate Michel and make sense of what was going on. Where was everyone? If they were fixing a wheel, she would hear them or at least see commotion around the carriage, but everything was eerily still and quiet.

Margaret sucked in a deep breath while she tightly wrung her hands in her lap. Should she get out and check on Michel? He had told her to stay in the carriage and wait, but she could not shake the nagging feeling that something was very wrong with the situation. She needed to know what was going on, and sitting in the carriage was not going to help her.

She placed her hand on the door handle and pushed it open. Just as she was about to step out, a hand grabbed her arm and Margaret gasped in shock.

"Get back in the carriage, Margaret. Something is not right. The driver is missing, and I cannot find him anywhere." Michel climbed in next to her and quickly shut the door.

"What about Randall, Jackie, and Henry? They were behind us, were they not?"

"They were when we left. However, their carriage is nowhere to be found."

"What do you think happened to them?"

"Most likely, we got separated from them. There were several carriages at the docks when we left, and it is possible they are just a further bit behind us."

"Should we wait, then?"

"No, the driver going missing makes me uneasy. On this stretch of the road, we are completely isolated."

"What are we going to do, Michel?"

"You are going to stay in here and I am going to take over as the driver and make sure we get home."

"Please do not go back out there. I have a horrible feeling about this."

Gently, Michel reached out and touched Margaret's face. He softly rubbed the side of her cheek with his thumb. "Margaret, I love you."

"And I love you, Michel."

He opened the carriage door and hopped down. He turned back around and smiled. "I promised I would protect you, and I mean it. Trust me."

But before Margaret could respond, a voice that made her immediately tremble with fear said, "Do not make promises you cannot keep."

Margaret screamed as one of the duke's hired mercenaries grabbed Michel and put a knife to his neck.

"Please, please, do not hurt him."

The duke grinned wickedly and threatened, "What I do to him depends on what you choose to do over the next several moments."

"What do you mean?"

"You know what I mean. I want my son."

"He is not here, and even if he were, you cannot have him."

"I am aware. Do you think I would leave any of this to chance? That is why I will be taking you with me." Witherton roughly grabbed her by the arm and yanked her down out of the carriage. "So you can get me my son. Of course, that is after we dispatch your 'fiancé' to make sure he does not come after us."

"He has nothing to do with this. Let him go."

"Now, we both know he cannot be left alive. 'No loose ends' is the motto I live by."

"Do not worry about me, Margaret. Save yourself," Michel yelled.

"Silly boy, there is no way out for her. She got the best of me during our last encounter, but I came prepared this time with help. I got rid of your driver and replaced him with my man here." He gestured to the man holding Michel at knife-point. "Then I made sure that your brother's carriage broke down and that you were separated on the road."

"You will never get away with this."

"My dear, you should know by now that I can get away with anything. I am the Duke of Witherton."

"You cannot go with him."

"Michel, if I can save your life by going with him, then that is what I am going to do."

"No, Margaret, listen to me. I do not care about myself. Your safety is all that matters to me."

"She is no longer your concern," the duke stated as he forced Margaret to walk towards his carriage.

"Kill him, and then get rid of the body and carriage."

"No!" Margaret cried out as she tried to break free and run back towards Michel, but the duke's grip was brutally tight, keeping her from reaching him.

"It is all right, Margaret. I love you." She could hear it in Michel's tone that he was saying goodbye, but she could not let herself accept it. She could not handle losing another person she loved.

Margaret watched in horror as the duke's henchman shifted the knife in his hand and started to push it into Michel's neck, but everyone was taken by surprise when Michel quickly jerked his head backwards and slammed it into the henchman's face.

The man stumbled backwards, dropping his knife, and grabbed his bleeding face in pain. Michel swirled away and pulled his sword free in one quick motion. Without hesitation, he thrust forward and sliced through the man's heart. The henchman slumped to the ground and suddenly stopped moving.

"My, my, are we not full of surprises," Witherton sneered as he unsheathed his own sword.

"I promised to keep Margaret and her son safe, and I always keep my promises."

"You will not be the first man she has loved who I have gotten rid of. I have become quite adept at it."

Without warning, the duke lunged forward and slashed at

Michel, who luckily was equally skilled in swordsmanship and successfully dodged the strike. He countered it with one of his own but was unable to land the blow. Both circled each other for several seconds, assessing how to attack the other effectively.

Margaret watched them with utter horror and could not help but recall the details she had been told about the duel between her late husband and Witherton. It had destroyed her life, and she knew how good the duke was because Henry had been excellent and he had still managed to best him. Michel was practiced, but she feared it would not be enough.

Out of the corner of her eye, Margaret noticed an object glinting in the sunlight several feet away. It was the knife that Witherton's henchman had dropped. She had to get to it. Trying to block out how the clinking sound of metal made her flinch and focus on her own task, she slowly made her way over to the knife and quickly picked it up. Keeping the knife in her hand, she placed it behind her and backed up until she was flat against the carriage.

Both men were getting winded as they continued to exchange blow for blow without landing a hit. Margaret was not sure how long they could go on before one of them dropped their guard and the other took advantage. She just prayed it was not Michel who ended up on the wrong end of the sword.

"You know, I could do this all day, but I am pressed to get

this finished so that I can take Margaret with me to get my son."

"I know you are trying to provoke me so that I will make a mistake. It will not work."

Witherton let out a cackle and spit out, "I do not need to provoke you to get what I want. All I have to do is wait you out. I am better than you, and we both know it."

"Your pride will be your downfall. You think too highly of yourself."

"And you have been made a fool by a woman with a ruined reputation."

"Nothing you say will change how I feel about Lady Margaret. I know everything that happened to her by your hands, and none of the vile things you say are true. You are just a bitter man with nothing of value in his life, chasing after a woman who clearly hates you."

The words must have struck a chord with the duke, as a look of pure rage crossed his face and he lunged at Michel full force. Michel stepped out of his way and turned around, and before Witherton could swivel around, Michel swung his sword and struck the duke in the shoulder, causing him to stagger forward and land on one knee. Intent on finishing the job, Michel advanced on Witherton and raised his sword.

Margaret inhaled sharply, expecting Michel to finally avenge the awful acts that the duke had done to her and her family. But Witherton was only faking being hurt to bait Michel in closer. Margaret saw that he still held his sword in his hand and was preparing to use it.

"Michel, watch out," Margaret yelled. However, it was too late. Just as the words left her mouth, Witherton spun around on one knee and swung upward with his sword, penetrating Michel right through the chest.

She fell to her knees and let out a scream. Then without warning, she began to sob uncontrollably and her whole body shook. It was all she could do to keep the knife in her hand and behind her back.

Michel crumpled to the ground, and Witherton pulled his sword free. He wiped the blade on Michel's clothing and then nonchalantly put the sword back in its sheath.

Determinedly, he walked over to Margaret and seized her by the arm and jerked her up, saying in a clipped voice, "Now that I have dealt with *that* inconvenience, it is time for us to go collect my son."

Margaret looked up at the duke and said, "Why must you always take away everything I love?"

Witherton sneered as he answered, "Because you belong to me. From the moment I laid eyes on you, I knew you were mine. I cannot stand the idea of you being with anyone else."

Margaret turned her head away, unable to stand looking at the man who had killed the two loves of her life. But the duke was not finished yet, reaching down to take her face in his hand. As he forced her to look at him, he continued, "I know, one day, you will see that I have done all of this for us and our family. You will love me again, Margaret. I swear it."

He was delusional. He actually thought he could

somehow find a way to make her love him. The man's arrogance knew no bounds.

Witherton reached down and touched her face with his fingertips, and then he slowly placed his lips on hers. Margaret went utterly still, afraid that if she moved at all, she would reveal the knife behind her back. Every inch of her revolted internally at the mere touch of him, and at any moment, he would sense her sheer disgust.

He whispered against her mouth, "Margaret, I have missed the taste of you so much."

Trying to block out the feelings that were coming back from when he violated her, Margaret forced herself to choke back the bile that was in her throat and concentrate on finding the right moment to attack.

"You feel it, the irresistible pull between us? We have always had this undeniable connection from the moment we met. We belong together."

Margaret glared up at Witherton and said, "I belong to no one." With one swift motion, she pulled the knife from behind her back and jabbed it into his side.

Witherton shrieked and lurched backwards, grabbing at his side, gasping in shock as he stared at her in disbelief. He stumbled a few more feet before falling to the ground.

She quickly ran past him without another thought. Michel was barely alive, his breathing ragged. Margaret dropped to her knees beside him and said, "I am here, Michel. You are going to pull through this, but I need to get you up." She put her arm under him and started to lift him up, but he cried out in pain.

"Do not move me. It hurts too much and will not do any good."

Gently, she laid his head in her lap and whispered, "I do not know what to do."

Michel whispered, "It is too late, Margaret. I am not going to make it." And then, almost as an afterthought, he asked in a worried tone, "Are you all right? Where is the duke?"

"I am all right, Michel. I took care of Witherton. We are safe now. I just need to get you to a doctor and he will be able to help you."

Michel shook his head. "There is no help for the wounds I have sustained." He coughed raggedly as more blood formed at the corner of his mouth. "I want you to know, these past few months with you have been the happiest of my life. My only regret is that I am leaving this world without being your husband."

"Michel, please do not say such things. I cannot bear it."

"Margaret, I need you to hear this. You and your son are the best things that have ever happened to me. I never knew I could love anyone as much as I love the two of you."

"What am I going to do without you, Michel? You are everything to me. I need you."

"You are strong, Margaret, so strong, and I know you *can* survive without me. You will for Henry's sake. I want you to make me a promise. I want you to leave Europe and never come back. Go to America like you had planned. Start over and do not let your past define you."

"I will, Michel. Whatever you want, I will do it."

His breathing was slowing down, and she could tell he was using every bit of strength to finish what he needed to tell her.

"I love you, Margaret." He reached out to touch her, and Margaret took his hand in her own.

"And I love you."

"Kiss me… one last time."

Margaret leaned down and pressed her lips to his. She lingered there for several moments before she realized that he was gone.

"No, no, no, no, Michel, please do not leave me. Please, do not go!" Huge sobs racked through her body as she became aware that the man who had broken through her defenses and helped her find a way to love again was dead. Everyone she loved, Witherton killed. And even though Witherton was also dead, it did not console her, nor make her loss easier to bear.

What was she going to do? She knew she needed to do something, but she could not make herself stand up.

God, give me the strength to get through this. I need you right now because I feel like I am going to break into a million pieces without Michel. I need your power to strengthen me and help me.

From behind her, she heard a noise that startled her. It was a rustling, and she jerked her head around to find Witherton stirring. He was not dead? She thought she had killed him; part of her wished she had. If he was not, she needed to run. He was hurt badly enough that she had a good head start, but she needed to get her family and leave on the next ship to America before he had a chance to recover.

Hurriedly, Margaret jumped to her feet and rushed to Michel's carriage. She unhooked and mounted the horse, saying a thankful prayer that she knew how to ride bareback. Her father had been furious when he found out that she had bribed the stable boy with sweet breads to teach her when she was eight. It turned out it was worth the whipping she had received back then as punishment.

"This is not over, Margaret," Witherton yelled through labored breathing. "You may think you are getting away, but you will never be free of me. I will always find you."

Choosing not to respond, because deep down she feared he might be right, Margaret galloped off in the direction of her estate.

CHAPTER 27

*L*ike Margaret had hoped, Randall had taken everyone back to their home. Quickly, she dismounted her horse and ran inside. She found Randall pacing back and forth in the parlor and Jackie sitting in one of the chairs.

Randall rushed up to his sister and grabbed her by the shoulders. "Margaret, what happened? Is everything all right?"

"No, everything is not all right," she said as she walked over to the window. She needed the comfort it always provided when nothing made sense and she felt lost. She stared out the window, hoping for something that could help her get through this.

"What do you mean, mon chéri? Where is Michel?" Jackie asked.

Without turning around, she whispered, "Michel is dead."

"Why? What happened?" Randall asked in confusion.

"It was Witherton."

"You mean he found you?" Jackie asked.

"He planned the whole thing. He followed us and he killed Michel."

"Oh no, Margaret. I am so sorry," Randall said as he went to his sister and placed an arm around her shoulders. "The driver knew something was wrong because the wheel on our carriage came off and it was not by accident. He must have planned for our carriage to break down, I think to separate us."

"Where is Witherton now?" Jackie asked.

"He is badly wounded, but I am not sure where he is or how long we have before he catches up with us. We need to leave for America as soon as possible."

"Everything is still packed, but Maggie, another ship does not depart until three days' time," Randall stated with worry in his voice.

"I know, so we need to go by carriage to the nearest port that has a ship leaving immediately."

"I will go find out the schedule for surrounding ports," Jackie said and quietly slipped out of the room.

"And I will go back to Michel's carriage, gather your belongings, and see if I can find any clues as to what happened to Witherton."

Margaret reached out and grabbed Randall by the arm. "Be careful, Rand. I cannot stand to lose one more person I love."

"I will, and I will not go alone. I will take Albert and a

couple of other servants with me."

Margaret nodded in agreement. "Can you also please bring Michel's body back here? I know we will not be able to stay to give him a proper burial, but I can at least make sure that he is not left out there all alone."

"Certainly."

Exhausted, Margaret wanted nothing more than to go to sleep, but she knew there was no time to rest. Time was of the essence with Witherton on their trail.

"Where is Henry?" Margaret asked with concern.

"He is safe up in his nursery."

"I am going to go get him ready to leave."

Randall nodded and then said, "I am so sorry, Maggie, for everything that happened today."

"It is not your fault, Rand. I thought we had enough time to get away. Then I made the mistake of thinking I could stay here and Michel would be able to protect us. I realize now, when it comes to Witherton, the only choice I have is to run."

"You did not know what was going to happen."

"You are right, but Michel is dead and it is because of my past catching up with me. I will not make that same mistake again. When we get to America, I am going to bury my past once and for all. Are you sure you are ready to walk away from our titles and life here?"

"You are my family, Mags, and wherever you go, I go. I lived without a title for almost half my life. This will be nothing new for me."

"Thank you, Rand. I do not know if I could do this without you."

"I will always be there for you, so you will never have to worry about that."

"I love you."

"I love you too."

Margaret was standing in front of a ship again. Two days later and three towns away, she was about to set voyage and finally leave her past behind. Her heart ached for the two men she loved and lost. Both died under different circumstances, but the cause of their deaths came from one common factor: Witherton. She hated him for what he had taken from her—first her trust, then her honor, and finally the loves of her life.

But a miracle happened that first night after Michel was killed. When she went up to get her son ready for their one-way trip to America, she found him sleeping. She looked at him and realized that not all was lost. He had gotten her through the death of her husband, and he would help get her through the death of Michel.

God had given her this perfect miracle in the form of her son, and she gathered him in her arms and walked over to the window. She looked out that window and saw a mother bird rebuilding a nest that had been destroyed by a windstorm. She realized that she needed to be like that mother bird and rebuild her own life. She needed to be strong so she could take care of her family instead of relying on a man to do it for her. And in order to find that strength, she needed to rely on God, because it was her faith that was going to get her through this season of loss.

And for the first time since she could remember, she felt true hope. Hope for a future that was unrestricted from the shackles of her past. Hope that she could build a life for her family that had meaning and was free from fear. Hope that what had been done to her would not define her. Hope was the gift God gave her in her darkest hour.

"Are you ready?" Randall asked, bringing Margaret back to the present.

Margaret turned to look at her twin and replied, "Yes. It is time for us to start our new life."

"Mon chéri, we have each other, and that is all that matters."

Margaret hugged her best friend. "I am glad you decided to still come with us."

"You have always been like family to me, and once I married Randy, we actually became family. I want to be wherever the both of you are," Jackie said with a loving smile.

Margaret's son ran up to her, grabbed her hand, and asked, "Bye-bye time, Mummy?"

She smiled down at her son and replied, "Yes, my darling, it is time for us to go make our new home."

"Michel with us?" Henry asked with hopeful expectation.

Margaret flinched inwardly due to the pain still being fresh from his death. She tried to hide her reaction by making herself hold the smile. "He is not going to be able to come with us, Henry."

"Oh," he said in a saddened tone, hanging his head in disappointment.

Margaret put her hand under her son's chin and raised it up so she could look him in the eyes. "It is going to be all right. He loved you very much, and I wish he could be with us, but he cannot. I love you, and Uncle Rand loves you, and Aunt Ja-Ja loves you. We are all going to be happy when we get to America."

Albert walked up to them and said, "Ma'am, it is time for us to board the ship now." Margaret nodded in acknowledgment, turned around to take one last look at France, and headed up the gangplank.

PREVIEW OF THE AMERICAN CONQUEST (BOOK 3)

1865 Port of New York, America

Margaret Learingam held on to the ship's rail with one hand and her toddler son with the other. As her family approached the New England shoreline, fear filled the pit of her stomach. Forced to flee to America, Margaret had no experience outside of Europe, where she had grown up in England and spent a year in France. She left everything behind, including her last name and titles, to keep her son from being taken away. And now, in just a few moments, she would be stepping foot into a new world that held the potential to offer her and her family a way to stay alive and together. It meant leaving behind her title, and the privileges that went with it, but she would do anything to protect her son.

Still haunted by the painful memories of losing the two

men she loved, Margaret could not help but feel guilt over their deaths. Her late husband and fiancé were both killed by the invidious hand of the Duke of Witherton.

Her heart was broken when her husband, Henry, the Viscount of Rolantry, was killed in a duel over her "ruined" honor. She had wanted to die with him, but when she realized she was pregnant, she knew she had to force herself to live for her child's sake. Fearful either the duke or her vengeful sister-in-law would take her son from her, Margaret fled from England to hide in France while she searched for her long-lost twin brother, Randall, whom she eventually found.

She thought she would never be happy after the tremendous loss of her husband, but she eventually found a way to live with the pain. When she met Michel, the Marquis de Badour, he showed her she could love again. But Witherton was not content to destroy her life only once; he had to do it again by killing Michel. In a cruel twist of fate, both men she loved were killed by the monster who had destroyed her life. After the second loss, Margaret shut her heart to the idea of finding love again, knowing the pain would be too crushing to warrant a third attempt. She had her son and brother, and they were the only two men she would need in her life.

The duke was still under the misguided assumption that her son, Henry, was his child, and he was determined to take him for himself. Knowing he would not stop until he got what he wanted, Margaret chose to leave behind her life in Europe and flee to America.

The trip across the Atlantic Ocean had been long and grueling, as they had encountered several storms in the process, lengthening their journey and causing sickness to run rampant on board. In addition, due to Margaret's appearance, she had been receiving constant unsolicited attention from the single men on the ship, which made her uncomfortable. Her dark violet eyes and long raven locks contrasted against her smooth white skin, and her petite frame had adjusted admirably into shapely proportions after childbirth. But she knew her attractiveness was not going to be able to save her when they reached the new land. In fact, she had the type of appearance that could get her into trouble.

Fortunately, she had a brother who gave up his life in France to keep her safe. Randall was her twin and, in some ways, the most important person in her life. Margaret had gone to France to search for him after he had been lost at sea eight years prior. The twins' physical features were similar in almost every way, but it was where their identicalness ended. Randall was outspoken and a reformed philanderer, while Margaret was more reserved.

Accompanying them was Jacquelyn, or Jackie, as her family called her. She would argue that she alone could claim to be Margaret's closest confidant. She was also Randall's newlywed wife. Jackie was a fiery strawberry blonde with golden-green eyes, whose second nature was to use her voluptuous body and personality to her benefit. Margaret still marveled at how their relationship was the catalyst for both of them to change their noncommittal ways. They made a fierce partnership.

Two loyal servants, Margaret's elderly butler, Albert, and personal servant, Sarah, chose to come with them. They were like family and had no ties to keep them in Europe. Together, all of them were going to forge a new life in the Colorado Territory with the land Margaret's deceased father secretly left her.

Many people had done it before them, had left their homes and lives behind to escape the law, poverty, or oppression. But she was fleeing to the new frontier in hopes of finding a place she could hide and never be found. Once and for all, she was going to leave behind all the hurt, humiliation, and horrible things that had happened to her in Europe.

During their oceanic journey, something amazing happened to Margaret's family. They met a preacher and his wife who were moving to America and wanted to start a church out west. And since the boat was mostly filled with young, unwed men moving to America to make quick and easy money, Pastor Nathan Thompson and his wife, Laura, decided it would be best to eat and socialize with Margaret and her family. Through their talks with them, Randall and Jackie came to know God, something Margaret had been praying for since she met Jackie and found Randall.

Margaret had accepted the Lord as her savior a couple years prior and wanted nothing more than to have the rest of her family feel the love, peace, and acceptance God offered.

As Margaret watched the transformation in Randall and Jackie, it was incredible to see the changes in their lives. They hungered to read the Bible, to ask Pastor Thompson questions about God, and to embrace everything entailing being a Christian. Margaret was pleased and excited as she realized that their entire family was truly starting a new life as they approached the New World. As an added bonus, Randall and Jackie's thirst to learn more about God kindled Margaret's faith in a new way, giving her a desire to become close to God like never before.

She smiled as she looked out at the approaching shoreline. This was going to be the start of their adventure to find their new home.

"Look at those docks. It is disgusting how they keep them. I cannot believe I followed you here."

Margaret rolled her eyes as she listened to her brother go on about how primitive the New World seemed to be. Personally, she found it fascinating. It was going to be so different than Europe. She had heard no one really paid attention to a person's class or their station in life here. It was as if everyone was equal. It was disturbing while intriguing.

"Oh, Rand, sometimes you are such a baby. You should be excited, like I am, about all the possibilities that this new place holds for us. Do you realize that here there are no titles or nobility? We are just like everyone else."

"You forget I only came into my title a few months ago. I barely got to use mine before I gave it up."

As they made their way down the gangplank, Jackie said, "Margaret is right, Randy. This place has charm." Jackie sniffed in distaste as a cart carrying dead fish was pulled by them. "Even if it is masked by repugnant, disagreeable bits and pieces."

"Well, Mags, what do we do from here?"

"Yes, Maggie"—Jackie had picked up Randall's habit of calling her by the nickname—"what is on the agenda?" she said in her noticeably thick French accent.

Margaret opened her parasol and placed it on her shoulder, saying, "We are going to get the supplies and men we need in order to join the wagons going west to the Colorado Territory."

"All right, but how are we going to afford that? Have you forgotten that we have no money?"

"I have a little bit left from what I saved up in France, and I have this." She pulled out the key that she had placed around her neck and hidden under her dress.

"Fetching necklace, my lovely sister, but what will *that* get us?"

She smiled slyly. "A few men who are willing to take the risk to see what is in our safety deposit box in Boulder."

"You have a safety deposit box there? How?"

"Father left it to me along with the deed to our land and new home."

"Well, what is in it?"

She shrugged. "I have no idea, but no one else knows that."

"We are going to promise American profiteers, who are just looking for an excuse to shoot up anything or anyone, money that we do not even know we have? I think the heat has gotten to you, because that is completely insane."

She tensed her lips. "No, it is completely brilliant. If nothing else, we can sell some of my dresses and jewelry in order to pay them."

He frowned. "You do not have any left. You sold the majority of your possessions to pay for our passage over here, as did we all."

"I still have Charlie." She thought of her expensive and precious mare that she had raised since she was a colt. The thought of selling Charlotte's Pride made her inwardly cringe, since she had staked her plans for a horse ranch in Boulder on the mare. "She could fetch a nice sum, I think."

She glanced down at her left hand and looked at the engagement ring her fiancé, Michel, had given her, then over at her other hand where she wore her wedding ring from Henry. "And I have my rings. They should help enough to get us to Colorado."

Randall shook his head. "No, I will not let it come to that. You will never have to part with your rings or your horse. It is all you have left. Not over my dead body."

"Then we have to go with my idea." She looked up from staring at her hands. "Besides, admit it. What really bothers you is that I came up with the plan, not you. You have always been the one to get us out of a tough spot, and it hurts your pride that I am going to do it this time."

"No, that is not it. I only—"

Tucking a piece of her curly strawberry blonde hair behind her ear, Jackie interrupted their argument. "All right siblings, quit squabbling. I think we need to move on now." She turned to Randall and said, "Unless you have a better idea, I suggest you be quiet. Now, let us go find a way to barter for our supplies."

As they made their way down the docks, Randall decided the best place to recruit men for their expedition would be at the nearest tavern.

"We are only going to have one shot at this, so let me do the talking. They will receive everything better from a man, and they will probably feel more comfortable striking a deal with me."

Margaret bit back her sharp reply that she was as good as any man and it was her money that he would be bargaining with, opting to say nothing instead. Even though she hated to admit it, it was true that Yankee men would receive the offer better from him. In the end, it might be the deciding factor.

"As you wish, Rand. But please, do not do anything that will compromise our position."

He winked at her. "I would not dream of it."

She said a silent prayer. *Lord, please help my brother not to wreck our chances at gaining the help we need to reach the Colorado Territory. He has a way of making things more difficult than they need to be, so please help him to handle this situation in a productive manner.*

~

Margaret could not believe things had come to this. She was standing in a Yankee tavern surrounded by harlots and scoundrels, and her own brother had deserted her in order to gamble away the last of their money.

She winced as she saw Randall lose another hand. No wonder her brother had owed so much money to so many hooligans back in France. He was a horrible poker player. Margaret, who was a woman and had played the game only a handful of times in her youth, could have had a better chance at winning than her brother.

Sighing heavily, she wondered what they were going to do. If he lost all their money, which it seemed he was bound and determine to do, then they were going to be worse off than they already were. It was time for her to intervene.

Margaret walked over from where she quietly had been watching to stand behind her brother. She put her hand on his shoulder and whispered firmly, "Rand, I think we should address the issue as to why we came in here."

He leaned his head back and glanced at his sister. He then returned his attention back to his hand. "Maggie, dear, I think that our luck is about to change."

She glanced at his cards and frowned in puzzlement. It had been such a long time since she had played cards. She had been seven and the stable boy had been teaching her how to play five-card draw. At least, until her tutor found out and put an end to it, saying it was "improper" for a well-bred young lady to play games of chance.

Struggling to remember what beat what, Margaret knew that four of anything was good, as well as sequenced numbers, especially if they were all the same color. But all her brother had was two pairs, both not being high numbers. She was quite sure that her brother did not possess a winning hand. She had to help him.

Margaret stared at her brother's cards and raised her eyebrows as if she were pleased with what she saw. Then she asked with an innocent voice, "Rand, are two kings and three queens good?"

There were murmurs around the table followed by several curses and shouts of anger. Then Margaret watched as four piles of cards were dropped to the table. They had all folded.

Randall smirked as he raked in the money that his sister had just helped him win. He stood up and grinned at the other men at the table. "I think we will take our leave from you."

Holding the newly acquired bag of American gold coins in his hand, Randall turned around and started to walk away. But before they could make their escape, a hand grabbed Randall's arm to stop him.

"Not with my money, you're not. You suckered us, boy, and that little gal of yours helped. I'm thinkin' I'm goin' to take my money back and then take out my anger on the both of ya."

Margaret watched as Randall tensed for a fight. She had not expected these rough Americans to take defeat so poorly. Poker could have only one winner, and tonight was not their night.

But now, it seemed her brother had won at the most inopportune time with a group that did not seem to take to outsiders, especially ones that beat them "at their own game" and took their money.

"I am sorry that you lost, but I need this money just as much as you do, if not more. Now, I will be leaving with both my money and the lady." Gradually, he pulled his arm free from the other man's grasp and pulled at the bottom of his jacket. "If you will excuse us, we must be on our way."

He turned and held out his arm for Margaret, but before she knew what was happening, she felt her brother fall away. She looked to the side and saw her brother grabbing his head. Someone must have hit him.

Randall quickly regained his balance and turned around, holding up his arms in defense. Margaret knew her brother was not about to go down without a fight. He would not want to be known for being taken down by a bunch of crazy Yanks.

He swung quick and hard, and the crack of his fist connecting with the other man's jaw resounded throughout the overcrowded tavern. The man staggered back but quickly recovered, showing he most probably had been in drunken poker fights before.

Just as the loudmouthed Yank pulled back to take another

swing, a voice interrupted the fight. "Bobby Budley, quit fightin' with the new fella. He won that money fair an' square an' ya know it. Let 'em be."

Bobby shuffled his feet, spit on the ground between them, and glared at Randall several seconds before stepping back. "Yer lucky that Johnny took a liken to ya, 'cause if he hadn't...." He let the thought finish itself. Everyone knew what he meant.

Randall wiped his brow with relief and turned around to face the man who had most probably saved their lives.

A burly man with shaggy brown hair and brown eyes, who looked like he had seen better times, greeted him. He smiled, showing a mouth with several teeth missing and an ugly gash that jaunted across his cheek.

"Name's Johnny Goodrich, an' I heard that yer looking fer a guide to the Colorado terr'tory. Seems lot o' people been wantin' to go there to get in on the s'posed 'Silver Rush.' Ya foreigners goin' fer that?"

"Yes, we need to go to Boulder, but not for the...," Randall answered, pausing awkwardly at the unknown phrase, "'Silver Rush.' We have some land there. Are you interested in taking the position as our head scout?"

The old Yank scratched his straggly beard and said, "'Pends."

"On what?"

"On how much ya payin'."

"Enough to make you exceedingly happy."

"How much might'n that be?"

"If you can get me a half dozen men, two wagons, oxen to pull the wagons, two additional horses and supplies, I will give you the winnings I just won."

The other man snorted and kicked the dust on the ground.

"That ain't enough to cover what me an' the boys cost, let alone supplies too."

"That, my fine fellow, is only a down payment. You will receive the rest when we all reach Boulder safely. And I can purchase the supplies, I suppose. Those winnings will be the down payment for 'you and the boys.' How does that sound?"

When Johnny frowned, Margaret started to worry until a smile crept across his face. "Now that sounds like a deal, partner. Be ready to move out in three days' time." He started to walk away, then turned back around. "Oh, an' be prepared for a heckuva trip. I hear the Cheyenne are on the warpath and are killin' up and down the Oregon Trail. It's gonna be a doozy of a time."

Margaret cautiously looked Johnny up and down, noting he did not look like one of the American cowboys she had heard about, but rather just the opposite. His round belly was an indication that he was extremely out of shape, which made her wonder how he had any chance of protecting them from highwaymen, much less Indians. But then, they did not have much choice in who to hire. They would have to take what they could get. She began to pray immediately. *God, please place a hedge of protection around us. We need you to keep us shielded during the long journey ahead. Only you can guard and keep us safe.*

Looking at her brother, Margaret saw her own worry reflected back in his matching violet eyes. Their faith in God would surely be tested in the months to come.

The American Conquest available now

ACKNOWLEDGMENTS

First and foremost, I am eternally grateful to Jesus, my lord and savior, who created me with this "writing bug" DNA.

In addition, many thanks go to:

My husband, Dustin, and three daughters, Katie, Julie, and Nikki, for loving me and supporting me during all my late-night writing marathons and coffee-infused mornings.

My mother, Connie, for being my first and most honest critic, now and always. As a little girl, sleeping under your desk during late-night deadlines for the local paper showed me what being a dedicated writer looked like.

My angels in heaven: my grandmother, who passed away in 2001, my infant son, Dylan, who was taken by SIDS three years ago, and my father, who left us this past year.

My good friend and fellow indie author, Alexia Purdy, who answered all my questions about this process and showed me the ropes. She also designed the stunning covers for *The Window to the Heart Saga.*

Hot Tree Editing and their beta readers for doing such an impeccable job preparing my writing for publication.

To my ARC Angels for taking the time to read my story and give valuable feedback.

To the Jenna Brandt Books Street Team, who have pounded the virtual streets on the internet, helping to spread the words about my books. Your dedication means a great deal.

ABOUT THE AUTHOR

Jenna Brandt graduated with her BA in English from Bethany College. She is an ongoing contributor for The Mighty website, and her blog has been featured on Yahoo Parenting, The Grief Toolbox, ABC News and Good Morning America websites.

Writing is her passion, with her focus in the Christian historical genre. Her books span from the Victorian to Western eras with elements of romance, suspense and faith.

Jenna also enjoys cooking, reading, and spending time with her three young daughters and husband where they live in the Central Valley of California. Jenna is also active in her local church, including serving on the first impressions team and writing features for the church's creative team.

A NOTE FROM THE AUTHOR

I hope you have enjoyed *The French Encounter* and plan to continue on this journey with Margaret in the final book of the series. Your opinion and support matters, so I would greatly appreciate you taking the time to leave a review. Without dedicated readers, a storyteller is lost. Thank you for investing in Margaret's story.

Jenna Brandt

Made in the USA
Columbia, SC
09 February 2021